ADAM SELZER

delacorte press

Copyright © 2009 by Adam Selzer

All rights reserved. Published in the United States by Delacorte Press, an imprint of Random House Children's Books, a division of Random House, Inc., New York.

Delacorte Press is a registered trademark and the colophon is a trademark of Random House, Inc.

Visit us on the Web! www.randomhouse.com/kids

Educators and librarians, for a variety of teaching tools, visit us at www.randomhouse.com/teachers

Library of Congress Cataloging-in-Publication Data
Selzer, Adam.
Andrew North blows up the world / Adam Selzer.—1st ed.
p. cm.
Summary: Ten-year-old Andrew North believes his father and brother are spies, and spends his time in middle school preparing to join the family business.
ISBN: 978-0-385-73648-0 (trade)—ISBN: 978-0-385-90611-1 (lib. bdg.)—ISBN: 978-0-375-89375-9 (e-book)
[1. Spies—Fiction. 2. Middle schools—Fiction. 3. Schools—Fiction. 4. Family life—Fiction.] I. Title.
PZ7.S4652And 2009
[Fic]—dc22
2009001659
The text of this book is set in 12-point Goudy.

Book design by Kenny Holcomb

Printed in the United States of America

10 9 8 7 6 5 4 3 2 1

First Edition

Thanks to the whole crew at
Olmsted Elementary in Urbandale, Iowa

For Ronni and Aidan

CHAPTERONE

Secret Agent Andrew "Danger" North moved like a cat through the Forbidden Zone. He ducked around piles of dirty clothes, hopped over stacks of used paper plates, and sifted through garbage. He needed every last one of his spy skills to find anything in a mess like this. All the years he'd kept his own room messy paid off regularly in his line of work.

But, like all good spies, even though his room was messy, his hair was perfect.

Beneath the papers that were piled in the corner, he saw it: the TC-99. To most people, it just looked like a really big calculator. But Agent North knew better. The TC-99 was a superpowerful spy gadget. He didn't know for sure what it could do, but he believed it could be used to shoot laser beams, send messages to headquarters, and, most likely, blow things up. North was determined to discover its secrets.

He gazed at the machine, with its big screen and strange buttons. Buttons like VARS, COS, and Y=. What could they possibly mean? Clearly it was some sort of spy code, but which of them would blow stuff up?

He would have to be careful, of course, but Agent North had never blown anything up that didn't deserve to get blown up. He dropped the TC-99 into his backpack and slipped out of the Forbidden Zone. The owner of the TC-99 would never even know he had been there . . .

Lying to Tony Zunker is probably the most popular sport in my whole school.

The day before the music program, someone told him he was on pace to break the world's record for Most Times Ever Getting Up to Sharpen Your Pencil in One Month. And he believed it.

I was pretending to pay attention in math class—but was really peeking into my desk to look at my brother's calculator—when Tony Zunker got up to sharpen his pencil again.

"How many are you up to today?" I whispered as he passed by.

"Twelve," he said.

Poor Tony. Lying to him isn't really much of a sport, if you ask me. He believes everything he hears!

Personally, I only believe stuff when I've thought it over and decided that it really makes sense. Like when my brother, Jack, told me that our dad is a spy and that he was training to be one, too, I didn't believe him at first. Who would? It sounded pretty crazy.

But then I started thinking about Dad. Sure, he has a huge collection of spy movies, and he loves to watch them with me and Jack, but lots of dads have those. What really tipped me off was his job. He tells people—including me—that he's an insurance salesman. But he can't even talk me into eating peas! How could he talk people into buying life insurance? Something strange was going on, all right.

That was when I started thinking about Dad's spy movies.

In those movies, all the spies have a fake job to tell normal people about—something that sounds really boring, like insurance salesman. That way, when the spy tells people he sells insurance, they don't say, "Oh, neat! Tell me more!" They just change the subject, because they're afraid that if they don't, he'll start trying to sell insurance to *them* or something, and they'll be bored to death.

I was beginning to feel like I was really on to something. But how could I be sure? I mean, clearly, Dad has to be really secretive about this whole thing, so he'd never admit it to me out loud. And he's really good about keeping all his spy gear hidden away—Jack says it's all hidden in a big secret chamber under our basement, and I've never been able to find it.

But one day, when I was digging through his desk, I found something that proved Dad is a spy! It was a bunch of old rings that had all these letters and numbers all over them. A whole stash of *secret decoder rings*!

I asked Dad what they were, just to see how he'd cover it up. He chuckled and said, "Oh, that's just my collection of old rings from cereal boxes."

Riiiiight. I knew the truth. Jack taught me this little bit of spy knowledge: when people chuckle before they say something like that, it usually means they're lying. Those rings were no cereal-box prizes. They were proof that I come from a family of spies!

Really, with a name like Andrew North, I was *born* to be a spy. It's a perfect name for a spy, or even a movie star, or the president, for that matter. It has that kind of ring to it. If Tony Zunker ever becomes a spy, he'll probably have to change his name, because no bad guys will get nervous when they hear that a guy named Tony Zunker is coming after them. But when they hear that Andrew "Danger" North is on their case, they'll know their days are numbered.

I'm pretty sure Jack got called up to the pros when he turned thirteen. Maybe it was a birthday present. Ever since then, he's spent all his time just hanging around in his room, acting really secretive. He stopped teaching me spy tricks and telling me weird secrets about our town, Cornersville Trace. I guess he's not allowed to now.

He told me a lot of weird secrets before. Like how Johnny Christmas, the rock star who died in 1979, isn't really dead at all. What *really* happened is that he got addicted to hot dogs and had to fake his death, because he was too embarrassed to go onstage when he couldn't fit into his jumpsuits anymore. He changed his name to Wayne Schneider and moved to the suburbs, where they'd never find him. He lives down the street from us now. It's awesome to know a secret like that. And I know it's true, too, because every time I walk past Mr. Schneider's house, I swear I smell mustard.

Mr. Summers, my teacher, didn't seem to notice that Tony was sharpening his pencil for the twelfth time that morning. Mr. Summers is a nice guy, but he'd never make it as a spy.

He *did* notice that I wasn't taking notes about math, though.

"Andrew?" he said, looking down at my paper. "Are you paying attention?"

"Sure I am!" I said.

"Well, make sure I see numbers on your page," Mr. Summers warned me.

See, he's a nice guy. He even lets us wear hats in class. He's young—younger than my parents, even. But I think that because he's so young, he hasn't learned that some of us just have too much on our minds to worry about division every day.

I really *was* taking notes, too. They just weren't about *math*. I was making notes on how I could get enough money to buy a pet monkey. All good spies have a sidekick, and monkeys make perfect assistants. They're really easy to train. But getting the money to buy a monkey wasn't going to be easy. Monkeys aren't cheap. Not anymore.

I also had notes on what to name the monkey once I got him. Some people think it's really cute to give monkeys a name like Bubbles or Mr. Chee Chee, but I'd give mine a regular name, like Dave. That would show the monkey that I respected him right away.

I knew I should probably get going on my long division, but I was having a hard time concentrating on anything that day. It was the day before the music program. That's when we have to sing a few of the songs we learn in Mr. Cunyan's music class in front of our parents. And this year, for the first time, I was going to be singing a solo. It's hard to concentrate on math with something like *that* on your mind.

Two minutes later, Tony got up again. This time, Mr. Summers noticed.

"Tony?" asked Mr. Summers. "Didn't you *just* get up to sharpen your pencil?"

"It's, uh, not as sharp as I like it to be," said Tony. "I don't like writing with a dull pencil."

Big mistake! Any spy would tell you that you have to create a believable lie if you want to get away with lurking around where you shouldn't be lurking. For example, if you want to get away with taking bonus trips to the pencil sharpener, you have to break the lead in your pencil first. No teacher can stop you from sharpening your pencil if the lead is broken. But Tony's just about as far from a spy as you can get. He's the worst liar in school. I guess that's because everyone else got good at it by lying to *him*, and he doesn't have anyone to practice on himself.

"He's gotten up about ten times, Mr. Summers," said Nicole Washington. "He's going for the world's record!"

Nicole Washington is sort of the boss of all the girls in class. She's one of those people who have never had a cavity, and she brags about it every chance she gets. If she were in one of my dad's spy movies, she would be the cop trying to foil the spy's mission at every turn so she could save the world herself. She *lives* to tell on people.

"Take your seat, Tony," said Mr. Summers. "There is no world record for sharpening your pencil."

"Yes there is!" said Tony.

If Tony kept talking like this, he was going to get in

trouble. I had to help. He was sort of a dork, but he was also one of my friends. Good spies take care of their friends.

"It's true, Mr. Summers," I said. "The world record for most times getting up to sharpen your pencil is four hundred forty in one month."

"Oh, really, Andrew?" said Mr. Summers. "Who in the world did that?"

"A guy named Mark Lane," I lied. "He was from Kenosha, Wisconsin. I think it was back in 1989."

Any time you need to name a city on the spot, you can count on Kenosha, Wisconsin. It can make almost any lie sound real. Dubuque, Iowa, works, too. Those are spy tricks that Jack taught me. He's a real genius.

"He's lying," said Neil Gorblisch.

I turned around and scowled at Neil, hoping Mr. Summers didn't ask anyone else's opinion. I knew most people would take Neil's side, not mine, because they knew that if they didn't, Neil might pound on them at recess.

Neil is just a plain old bully. If *he* were in one of my dad's spy movies, he would be the guy who the head villain sends out to do all his dirty work. The *real* villains never beat up anyone themselves—they hire goons like Neil.

Luckily for me and Tony, Mr. Summers ignored Neil.

"Well, I'm sure that Mark Lane's teacher must have been very proud of him," he said. "And I am, too, because he's just given me a great idea for a math problem!"

Mr. Summers is a math nut. If the principal, Mrs. Wellington, got on the intercom and said, "Attention, students: the world will end in five minutes," he would probably say, "Oh boy! Let's figure out how many seconds there are in five minutes!" That's how crazy he is about math.

He pulled out a blue marker and wrote "440" on the marker board.

"Now," he said, "how many days are we in school each month?"

"About twenty," said Nicole, as if Mr. Summers didn't already know that.

Being a teacher must be really boring. You have to spend all day asking questions that you already know the answers to. Plus, you never get to jump out of airplanes. And only science teachers ever get to blow things up.

"Right. We'll go with twenty," Mr. Summers said, writing that on the board, too. "So, if we're in class twenty days per month, how do we find out how many times per day Mark Lane must have sharpened his pencil?"

"It's four hundred forty divided by twenty," said Nicole. "And the answer is twenty-two."

"That's right!" said Mr. Summers. "Old Mark must have gotten up to sharpen his pencil twenty-two times every day that month. Very good, Nicole! Now, let's see how many times per hour that is. This is gonna be a tough one! We're in school six and a half hours per day, so it's twenty-two divided by six and a half. This is really at *least* fifth-grade math, so pay attention!"

Mr. Summers spent the next twenty minutes turning my lie into math problems. After we figured out that Mark had sharpened his pencil 3.38 times per hour, we figured out that that was once every 17.75 minutes. Then someone pointed out that we were only actually in *class* four and a half hours a day, since lunch, recess, and stuff like music, gym, and art took up two hours per day, and Mr. Summers started all over again. He looked like he was having the time of his life. He even asked Tony to sharpen his pencil a few more times so we could find out how many times you have to sharpen a pencil before it's worn down to a nub. Then he used division and found out how many pencils Mark Lane must have gone through.

Later on, when we were all doing worksheets, Tony leaned over to me. "Nice job of saving my butt!" he said.

"Don't mention it," I said.

"But you know what?" he asked. "If I kept at it, I bet I could have sharpened my pencil at least thirty times today. That's *way* more than that Mark Lane guy was doing it!"

I'll bet that the used-car store on Eighty-second Street has a car set aside for when Tony turns sixteen: an old broken-down one that's worth about as much as his bike. They'll tell him it's a classic that some old lady owned just to drive it to church once a week, so it's still in perfect shape. And he'll believe it.

Luckily for Tony, I'm planning to be a billionaire by the time I turn sixteen. I'll have enough money to buy really fancy sports cars for both of us. Maybe even one for Dave the Monkey. They'll be top-of-the-line, superfast machines with built-in TVs, fish tanks, candy machines, periscopes, and ejection seats. After I join the family business and become a pro spy, I'll need a car with an ejection seat for sure.

I was ready to go pro. I just had to find a way to let headquarters know. And I had the perfect tool to do it.

I had "borrowed" it from Jack's room that morning while he was in the shower. Jack called it his calculator, but a spy like me could see that it was no calculator. It was about the size of a brick, and it was covered with buttons that didn't make any sense. It had letter keys, not just number keys. And the screen was so big that it could probably show pictures.

It was obviously a spy gadget of some sort. If I typed in a message, I figured it would get beamed back to headquarters. I had to be really careful with it, though, because if I pushed the wrong button, it might explode. Seriously. You can't be too careful with spy gadgets.

Maybe I shouldn't have stolen the calculator. Maybe I should have just been patient and waited till I was thirteen and headquarters contacted me, like they contacted Jack. But let's face it: I was a lot smarter than your average kid. I mean, I had put all this stuff together on my own. It was a waste of serious spy talent not to use me, even if I was only nine. A kid like me could save the world.

Besides, once I was in training like Jack, we could hang out together like we used to, back before he went pro. I really missed hanging out with him.

So after I finally finished my math worksheet and handed

it in, I took out the calculator. Using the letter keys, I typed in `This is Andrew North, Jack's brother. I am ready to go pro. Come see me at the music program at Cornersville West Elementary tomorrow night!`

I looked for a SEND button that would beam my message straight into headquarters. I couldn't find one, though, so I tried hitting a whole bunch of buttons at once.

All of a sudden, the screen went *nuts*! All the letters disappeared, and little black flashing dots showed up in their place! Then the word `Working` started flashing on the screen.

I started to get nervous. What had I done? What if I pushed the wrong button, and instead of sending the message, I'd set the thing to self-destruct? Or, worse, what if I had accidentally punched in a code that would launch a whole bunch of missiles right at Moscow? Had I just started World War III?

I was starting to have some serious second thoughts. Maybe I wasn't ready to be a full-fledged spy. Maybe I should have left the calculator, or whatever it was, with Jack— someone who actually knew how to use it!

I started pushing buttons like mad, trying to get it to stop. Nothing happened; it just kept saying "Working." Finally, I turned the thing upside down, opened the case, and took out the batteries. Then I breathed a sigh of relief—I'd narrowly saved everyone from getting blown up, and they'd never even know it!

That was the kind of on-my-feet thinking the spy head-quarters would be lucky to get!

But when I looked up, everyone was staring at me.

"You aren't allowed to use calculators in class, Andrew," said Nicole.

"I'm not!" I said. "I already turned in my worksheet!"

"Andrew," said Mr. Summers, who was walking over to my desk, "you know I don't allow calculators. I'm teaching you guys to do math with your brains!"

Mr. Summers is really big on doing math with your brain. He even has a rubber hand in his desk that he claims he cut off some kid when he saw him counting on his fingers to do subtraction. I think only Tony Zunker believes that one.

"I didn't use it for class," I said. "I was just experimenting with it."

Mr. Summers picked up the calculator and looked at it. "This is a nice one," he said. "But it's really for algebra and stuff, not third-grade math. And you know these aren't allowed, anyway. I'm going to have to take this for the weekend."

"No!" I said. "You can't!" It was only *Thursday*. Surely Jack would notice it was gone! And what if he needed it to warn headquarters about some shark-loving billionaire who liked to coat people in gold or something?

"Sorry, Andrew," Mr. Summers said. "Those are the rules. You can have it back on Monday."

He took the calculator and put it into the top drawer of his desk with the rubber hand.

This was really bad. Even if Jack somehow didn't notice it was gone, Mr. Summers *was* a math nut. There was a pretty good chance that he might pick up the device to do some algebra over the weekend—just for fun! I knew enough to take the batteries out if the thing looked like it was gonna blow, but Mr. Summers didn't know it was a spy gadget. He might accidentally punch in a code that would blow up the whole school—maybe the whole town! Or the world! Maybe the world would end before school even let out! And it would be my fault. I could just imagine the newspaper headlines if the newspapers didn't all get blown up. They'd say: *Andrew North Blows Up the World!*

Even if we *did* survive the afternoon, if Jack found out the calculator was gone, he'd kill me!

I had to get that calculator back, and fast!

CHAPTER**TWO**

Andrew "Danger" North took in the strange woman who stood before him. Her gruesome stare burned into his skin—even though her left eye was covered by a patch. The scar on her cheek reminded him that she knew how to fight. It also reminded him of the famous scar above Dr. Cringe's eyebrow. Could this woman be working for Dr. Cringe?

Agent North moved closer to her. Behind her, the clang of metal against metal created a sort of symphony. There were dozens of knives visible behind her, and North was aware that she knew how to use them.

But Agent North hadn't come to fight. He had come to eat.

"Whattaya want, honey?" she asked him. "The Salisbury steak and potato salad, or the three-bean casserole and potato salad?"

You can do a lot of different things with potatoes. You can bake them, mash them, or make them into French fries. But in the school cafeteria, it seems like the only thing they know how to do is make them into cold potato salad, because that's the way they serve them every day. People who eat the hot lunch probably get about five times the recommended daily allowance of mayonnaise.

Maybe some powerful potato-salad company is bribing the principal. That sort of thing happens sometimes, you know. Some big rich guy will show up in the office and say, "Listen, buddy! My brother is a potato-salad salesman, and you're going to buy potato salad from him to serve in the cafeteria every day, or we'll beat you up and bash in your headlights. Got it?" Maybe one of my first missions when I become a professional spy will be to break up the potato-salad racket.

Since it was Thursday, I wasn't about to eat the stuff, because I know for sure they make it on Monday and serve us the same batch all week. Jack told me that when I first started school. Having a spy for a brother comes in handy. Unlike most of the kids, I know that I should never eat it after Wednesday.

I sat down at a lunch table next to Tony Zunker, Danny Nelson, and Paul Hazuka. We were all friends, but we only saw each other at lunch and recess, because Danny and Paul were in Mrs. Burgett's class.

"I'm thinking of skipping recess," I said as I sat down. "We could all be in real danger."

"Because Mr. Summers took your calculator?" asked Tony.

"It's not mine, it's Jack's!" I said. "And it's not just an ordinary calculator—it's a spy gadget! If Mr. Summers starts fiddling with it, it might explode!"

"He'll fiddle with it, all right," said Tony. "He might be using it to do some math right now!"

It may seem strange that I told my friends I come from a spy family. Jack told me not to tell anyone, but by the time he told me that, I'd kind of already let it slip to Paul, Danny, and Tony. They've done a really good job of keeping my secret, though. They may not be spy material, but they're definitely on the right side. I figure I can train them all to be my assistants someday. They can clean my suits and talk about insurance with me in public. All spies need guys like that. Even Batman needs his butler and that guy who makes all his gadgets.

"Seriously?" asked Danny. "Your brother has a calculator that can blow people up?"

"It can probably blow up the whole *town*!" I replied. "Maybe even the world!"

"Awesome!" said Danny.

Danny wears camouflage a lot, even though there's no forest or anything to blend into around school. He's also really into weapons. One time when he and I were in the same art class, we had to use egg beaters to mix up paint. He got in big trouble after Mr. Murrell caught him waving the egg beater around and saying, "I wouldn't want to be the next guy whose head I crack open! I'll scramble his brains!" As far as I know, Danny's never actually cracked anyone's head open before, but he does get sent to talk to the guidance counselor *a lot.*

Paul rolled his eyes at me. He's a real champion eye-roller.

"Your brother isn't a spy," he said. "Give it up."

"He is too!" said Tony.

"Ignore him," I whispered to Tony.

Tony, Danny, and I know that a lot of strange things go on in town, but Paul Hazuka doesn't believe any of it. He also doesn't believe in ghosts, or aliens, or the Loch Ness Monster, or anything like that. I'll bet he grows up to sell insurance for real.

I mean, any idiot can see that there are strange things going on in our town if they just look around a bit. For instance, in the middle of the mall, right near the food court, there's a life-sized statue of a naked guy with angel wings riding a tricycle. You can see his butt and everything. There has to be a secret spy chamber under that statue. Why else would anything that weird be right in the middle of the mall? But Paul just thinks it means that the owner of the mall has weird taste in art. He's never going to save the world thinking like that.

"So, where did Mr. Summers put it?" asked Danny.

"It's in his desk," I said.

"That's no big deal," said Danny. "You can probably get it back from there."

"Sure," I said. "It's nothing I can't handle."

"Yeah," said Danny. "I was afraid you were going to say he put it into Storage Room B!"

"That room where they take stuff that isn't claimed from the Lost and Found?" Tony asked.

Danny nodded while he sipped his milk. "Yeah," he said. "It's also where they put stuff that gets taken up for the whole year. Mr. Gormulka guards that room with his life!"

I gulped. Mr. Gormulka, if that is in fact his real name, is the janitor—or so he wants us to believe. The story goes that he fought in some war a long time ago, and when he came back, all he wanted in life was to help keep America clean, so he got a job as a janitor. But I'm pretty sure he's a criminal or a spy or something. He sure *looks* like a criminal. He's always sort of grumpy, and he has this nasty scar above his left eyebrow that looks like the letter "M." When he raises his eyebrow, the scar moves, almost like a bat flapping its wings. It's really freaky.

He hates my guts, too. I puked in the hallway once in kindergarten, and I don't think he ever quite forgave me. He's always walking around the halls, looking all creepy and whistling. Whistling makes some people seem happy, but with Mr. Gormulka, it's about the creepiest thing ever.

"You think he's hiding something in there?" I asked.

"Duh," said Danny. "That's, like, common knowledge."

"I've always heard that there are a ton of comic books in there," said Paul. "But I'll bet there's nothing in there but old mittens."

"There are comic books, all right," said Danny. "There's

a collection in there worth about a million dollars, and they all got lost around the school. Every time someone loses one or gets a comic book confiscated, Mr. Gormulka keeps it."

"No kidding?" I asked. Jack had never told me that!

"And that's not all," said Danny. "There are *dead bodies* hidden in that room!"

"Get real," said Paul, who rolled his eyes again.

"I'm serious," said Danny. "I think they're the bodies of kids who died from jumping off the top of the slide or doing dangerous stunts on the monkey bars. The school hid the bodies and told the parents they ran away so they wouldn't get sued!"

"I've heard that, too," said Tony.

"I doubt that's true," I said. Sometimes my superspy skills help me tell when something doesn't make any sense. "If the school wanted to cover up that a kid died on the playground, they'd probably bury them under the cafeteria or something. Someplace where no one would find them. And anyway, Jack would have told me about that."

"You guys are stupid," said Paul. "If there were dead bodies under the cafeteria, they'd start to stink."

"Who would notice?" said Danny. "The cafeteria stinks all the time."

"Look," said Paul. "Be realistic. Your brother's calculator is just in a desk, not in some hidden chamber full of dead bodies. If you want to get it back, just get in trouble."

"What?" I asked.

"Get yourself in just enough trouble to get an indoor

recess," said Paul. "Then wait until Mr. Summers goes to get more coffee from the teachers' lounge and grab it out of his desk. Piece of cake."

"Hey," I said, perking up. "That's not a bad idea."

Paul shrugged. "Honestly, Andrew," he said. "If you stopped pretending to be a spy and started thinking like a normal person, you could come up with stuff like this yourself!"

It really *was* a good plan—simple and elegant. I had been thinking of maybe mixing up glue, some of the potato salad, and some of the cleaning supplies under the drinking fountain and finding a way to set fire to it in the bathroom. When it started to stink, people would think there was a gas leak, and when they marched everyone outside, I could run into the classroom and grab the calculator. Paul's idea was a lot easier. After all, the only way I could start a fire in the bathroom was by rubbing two sticks together, and that's really hard to do.

Just then, Neil Gorblisch sat down at our table. I never like to sit by Neil. In addition to being a bully, he's a pretty gross eater. If I were a pig, I'd insult the other pigs by saying that they ate like Neil Gorblisch. That's how gross he eats.

"Well, well," he said, looking around at us. "Look who's here! The geek gang!"

"Of course we're here, cheese bag," I said. "It's school! We're here every day."

"Cheese bag?" asked Neil. "What's a cheese bag?"

"You are," I said.

Actually, I had no idea what a cheese bag was, but it was a pretty good insult. I bought it off Ryan Kowalski, the class criminal. Ryan is sort of a genius when it comes to making up insults. You know how professional spies have guys who make their weapons and gadgets for them? Ryan is a bit like that guy for me. I can't take weapons to school, of course, but I can take insults. Give him fifty cents, and he'll write you a pretty choice put-down.

Neil curled his lip at me. He thinks he looks very threatening when he curls his lip. Actually, he sort of does.

"Shut up, An-dy," he said.

I gave him my own meanest look. "What did you call me, Gorblisch?" I asked.

"You heard me," said Neil. "An-dy!"

That did it!

No one, but no one, calls me Andy!

Andrew North is a great spy name, but Andy North isn't. That sounds like the name of a trucker who takes too long in the bathroom. Or a professional bowler who does commercials for toe-fungus cream. I don't let anybody call me Andy, and Neil knows it.

"Oh yeah?" I asked. "At least my last name doesn't sound like the noise a toilet makes when you flush it! Goooorrrrrblisch!"

Tony started laughing. So did Danny and Paul. Ryan had charged me a whole dollar for that insult, but it was worth it.

"Shut up!" said Neil. "You're a dork, North!"

"Back to you and more of it!" I said.

Neil dug his spoon into his potato salad and made a move like he was going to fling it at me.

Naturally, I sprang into action. Before he could do anything, I dug my spoon into my own potato salad and flung it at Neil. It hit him square on the nose, then hung there for a second like a giant booger before dropping onto his plate.

Neil growled. Then he scooped up some of his potato salad and lobbed it at me. It hit me in the chest and clung to my shirt.

Tony Zunker grabbed a spoonful of his potato salad and reached up to throw it, but he never had a chance. Mrs. Rademacher, the lunchroom monitor, showed up behind him before he could let it fly.

"What's going on here?" she asked in that tone of voice adults use to tell you that someone's about to get into trouble.

"He threw potato salad at me," Neil grumbled.

"And he threw it at me!" I said, pointing at Neil. "And he started it, too."

"Did not!" Neil lied.

"Andrew started it, Mrs. Rademacher," said Nicole. She was sitting at the next table over, where she had been bossing around a group of girls. "I saw the whole thing. Tony was about to throw some, too."

"Thank you, Nicole," said Mrs. Rademacher. "Come with me, Andrew and Tony."

She grabbed our shoulders and led us down the hall. She was awfully strong for someone as old as she was. And awfully mean. And thanks to her, who knew whether I'd be able to put Paul's awesome Indoor-Recess Calculator-Retrieval Plan into motion today?

"This is so unfair!" I said. "Tony shouldn't be in trouble!"

"I didn't even throw anything!" said Tony. "Neil did!"

But being fair was not something Mrs. Rademacher was known for.

"Poor Neil was just defending himself from you hooligans!" said Mrs. Rademacher. "You'll be spending your recess indoors, in your classroom!"

Sweet.

Tony nudged me and smiled. I smiled back. Although we were in trouble for totally unfair reasons, it was my perfect chance to get the calculator back before Mr. Summers could blow up the world!

CHAPTER THREE

Madam Mordre, the evil Dr. Cringe's equally evil assistant, led Agent North down the corridor, handcuffs chafing his wrists. Dave the Monkey followed along in tiny handcuffs of his own.

North's plan was working perfectly! He had intended to fight his way into Dr. Cringe's chambers but realized that if he lost the fight on purpose and let them simply capture him, Madam Mordre would lead him right into the chamber! As soon as she looked away, he would break free of the handcuffs.

His suit was a bit messed up from the fight, but his hair was still perfect.

Madam Mordre grinned as she led North through the door into the secret chamber, where Dr. Cringe was waiting.

"Come on," she said. "You'll be spending your recess in here."

Mr. Summers was sitting at his desk, grading our worksheets and listening to music on headphones, and Ryan Kowalski was leaning his chair back and putting his feet up on his desk. Ryan had to eat his lunch in the classroom every day. No one knew what he'd called Mrs. Rademacher to get permanent indoor recess, and he wasn't telling.

"Got two more for you," said Mrs. Rademacher.

"Oh?" said Mr. Summers, looking up.

"Yes," said Mrs. Rademacher. "They'll be spending the rest of lunch and recess indoors with Ryan. And Ryan, put your feet down!"

"Sure thing, Mrs. R," said Ryan.

Mr. Summers nodded and gestured for us to have a seat. I sat down next to Ryan, and Tony sat down next to me.

Ryan was dressed in a plain white T-shirt with the sleeves rolled up. His hair was slicked back, and he was chewing on a pencil.

"What are you guys in for?" Ryan asked.

"Throwing potato salad at Neil," I said proudly.

Ryan nodded. "Looks like Neil got you back, too." He pointed at my chest.

"Guess so," I said. "Are we allowed to talk out loud in here?"

"Sure," said Ryan. He turned and started talking really loudly so Mr. Summers could hear him through his headphones. *"Mr. Summers doesn't mind if we talk here. Do you, Mr. S?"*

"Knock yourselves out," said Mr. Summers. "I'm not a jailer. I'm just here to make sure you don't break the windows and write dirty words on the marker board."

And he went back to grading papers and listening to his headphones.

"Hey, Ryan," I said, quietly enough that Mr. Summers wouldn't hear, "that insult you gave me about Neil's name sounding like a toilet flush worked really well!"

"I knew it would," said Ryan. "Need any more?"

"Not today," I said, "but as soon as I get some cash, I'll buy a whole bunch."

"Whenever you're ready," he said. "I'm having a sale this month—five insults for only two bucks."

I needed to do something to get some more money. I really did need more insults, but I didn't know how much I could afford to spend, considering I had a monkey to save for. Of course, if I had managed to contact spy headquarters and they called me up to the pros, I'd be able to afford a monkey and a *ton* of insults!

The whole time we talked, I kept a close eye on Mr. Summers. I knew he had to get up some time, which would give me a chance to get the calculator back. If he didn't leave the room, I was going to have to find some way to get all of us out of the room, which was going to be a real trick.

After lunchtime ended and everyone else was out on the playground, Mr. Summers gave us some drawing paper to keep us occupied during our indoor recess. I drew a blueprint for the house where Jack and I would live after we had both gone pro as spies. It would have everything—giant TVs, a swimming pool the size of a football field, a video-game room, and maybe an indoor baseball stadium. It would even have private suites in the basement for Tony and Danny, my assistants. There would be secret passages all over and a telescope on the roof that we could use to look into windows all over town.

Paul Hazuka could live there with us, too, even though he'd probably never believe we were spies. He'd probably think we made all our money from "good investments" or something and that I just dressed so sharply to impress the ladies (which would only be half true). But that would be okay—if anyone came snooping around, he could answer the door and say, "Spies? No, no spies here. Nobody here but us insurance salesmen!"

While I worked on a design for the monkey habitat where Dave would live, I thought about all the stuff Danny had said about Storage Room B. Jack had never told me anything about it, so I sort of doubted there was anything *that* secret in there. But it was possible. Anything is possible in a town like Cornersville Trace.

"Hey," I said to Ryan. "Did you ever hear any stories about Storage Room B?"

Ryan spent more time in the school than anybody, since he got detention so often. If anyone knew anything, it would be him.

"Oh yeah," he said, nodding. "I've heard a lot about that

room. There's supposed to be some really valuable stuff in there."

"Yeah, I've heard that," I said. "Might be worth a look."

"You'll never get a look in the place," said Ryan. "Mr. Gormulka is insane about keeping it guarded. Man, I've sure heard some scary stuff about *that* guy!"

"Yeah?" I said.

"Heck yeah," Ryan said. "You hear crazy things when you're stuck in this place, man. Terrible things. I've heard things in here that are going to haunt me to the grave."

"Like what?" I said.

He gestured for us to lean in closer. "Well," he said in a low voice, "you've heard how Gormulka became a janitor after fighting in some war, right?"

"Sure," I said. "Everyone's heard that."

"Well, that's partially true. But the thing is, he wasn't fighting for America. He was fighting for the Russians during the Cold War! And he still works for them, just undercover. Now that the Cold War is over, his spy team works for anybody who can pay."

"Really?" I asked.

Tony leaned over my desk. His eyes were as wide as dinner plates.

"For sure," said Ryan. "You know that scar over his eye that looks like an 'M'? That's not just a scar. It's the mark of the group he works for. From what I've heard, he thinks that one of the teachers here, or maybe even one of the students, is actually a spy. And he's just waiting to find out who it is.

As soon as he finds out, that person is as dead as a drain-
pipe!"

"Oh my God!" said Tony.

He kicked my shin under the desk, like I needed to be
reminded that there *was* a spy in the school: me!

"You can't be serious," I said, trying not to freak out.

"I am," said Ryan. "So if I were you, Tony, I'd be really
careful about the pencil-sharpening thing. If Mr. Gormulka
finds out you have skills like that, he might decide *you're*
the spy!"

The wheels in my head were turning. Maybe defeating evil
Mr. Gormulka could be the job I did to prove that I was
ready to be a professional spy! But, on the other hand, they
don't send spies in to fight bad guys without a whole bunch of
cool gadgets. If Mr. Gormulka was really an evil spy, I wasn't
about to fight him without a special ring that shot out laser
beams that could freeze him into a statue or something. Who
knew what sort of weapons he might have in Storage Room
B? Maybe he even had a shark tank in there!

Just then, Mr. Summers took off his headphones and
stood up. "You guys sit tight," he said. "I have to go to the
teachers' lounge to get more coffee. I can trust you guys to behave for a minute and a half, right?"

"Sure thing, Mr. S," said Ryan.

"Good," said Mr. Summers. "You guys are on the honor
system. If I see a single dirty word on the marker board, you're
all dead meat!"

Mr. Summers smiled and walked out of the room. Now, I knew I'd promised not to do anything wrong, but as any spy will tell you, sometimes it's okay to break the rules. Like when the world might blow up if you don't. This was one of those times. It was a perfect chance to get the calculator back and save the world!

I jumped out of my seat and walked up to Mr. Summers's desk, where the calculator was in a drawer. I opened the drawer, grabbed the calculator, and hopped back to my desk. Mission accomplished!

"That's one big calculator," said Ryan.

"It's my brother's," I said really casually so he wouldn't know I'd probably just saved the world from getting blown up. If he knew *I* was the spy, he might let it slip to Mr. Gormulka under torture or something.

"Wow," said Ryan as he looked the calculator over. "What does the Y= button do?"

"I don't know," I said. "I'm still trying to figure the thing out. But if I don't get it back home before Jack knows it's gone, I'm dead. Promise you won't tell Mr. Summers I got it back from his desk?"

"Sure," said Ryan. "I'm no tattler."

I went back to work fiddling with the thing, trying to make sure no secret message had been beamed into it while it was in Mr. Summers's desk. All I saw on the screen when I turned it on was the message I'd typed in before. The screen wasn't going nuts anymore; the flashing black dots were gone. I breathed a sigh of relief, found the OFF button, and pushed it. The screen went blank, which I guess meant that the world was safe.

I was just about to put it away when Mr. Summers came back into the room.

"Andrew?" he said. "Please tell me you didn't break into my desk to get that!"

"Sorry about that," I said. I tried to smile and chuckle a little bit like people always do when they get caught lying. It never works, but I couldn't very well have told him that it just *flew* out of his desk or anything!

It would have been pretty cool if it had, though.

Mr. Summers walked over and took the calculator from me. "I'm going to have to put it someplace safer for the weekend," he said. He stepped out into the hall and shouted, "Excuse me, Hank!"

I heard the sound of footsteps coming down the hall, and a second later, Mr. Gormulka was standing in the doorway. He glared in at us. I could see his M-shaped scar from clear across the room!

"Got a confiscated item for the weekend," said Mr. Summers. "Can you put this in Storage Room B until Monday?"

Mr. Gormulka nodded and took the calculator without a word, then disappeared into the hall. I could hear him whistling as he walked away.

"Oh man," Tony whispered. "You're a goner!"

I began to panic. Mr. Gormulka, being an evil spy

himself, would probably recognize that the calculator was a spy gadget. And as soon as he turned it on and saw my message, he'd know who the spy in school was!

If what Ryan said about Mr. Gormulka was even *halfway* true, I was as good as dead!

CHAPTERFOUR

None of the other people gathered around the piano knew that the kid with the perfect hair and the really sharp suit, the one with a voice like an angel, was really Andrew "Danger" North, international superspy. As far as they knew, he was Thaddeus Arthur III, the wealthy heir to the Arthur Badminton Equipment fortune, who had arrived at the party unannounced and thrilled the other wealthy guests with his incredible musical talent.

Little did they know that when Thaddeus sang the next song, the high note in the bridge was the signal for Dave the Monkey, his trusted companion, to arrive on the scene and throw a net over Dr. Cringe, the oil executive who was secretly plotting the destruction of the United States and who was watching the whole party from the balcony, wearing a hat to cover up his famous scar. . . .

It was too bad I didn't have a monkey yet. Everyone knows that monkeys are natural lock pickers, and I could sure have used some help picking the lock of Storage Room B. But even if I could get the lock open, getting the calculator out of there might not be easy. I knew that if he caught me, Mr. Gormulka might *kill* me! And even if he didn't, I could fall into a shark tank the second I stepped inside. Or a spider tank, maybe. Those are even worse than shark tanks. He probably had the room rigged with all *kinds* of booby traps.

I was so caught up with worrying about getting the calculator back that I almost forgot about the music program coming up until we went to music class. We had music on Tuesday and Thursday afternoons and gym the other days, so this would be our last class before the program the next night.

Mr. Cunyan, the music teacher, had been teaching music at the school ever since it opened. He was probably pretty young then, but now he was really, really old. He had a face that looked like a crescent moon when you saw it from the side—his chin and nose stuck out more than most people's. He also had so many wrinkles that I was afraid one day he'd just turn inside out.

The first song we were singing as a class was called "Hello Central, Give Me No Man's Land." It's what they call a "parlor song": an old song about a dumb kid who tries to call his dad on the phone, even though his dad had died fighting in World War I. Mr. Cunyan says he used to sing it when he was a kid. If any kid went around singing a

36

song that depressing nowadays without a teacher making them sing it, they'd get sent to the guidance counselor for sure.

"Okay, everybody," said Mr. Cunyan. "Now, I know that 'Hello Central' is a sad song, but I want you smiling really big. In the song, you're just little children, not big children, like you are right now. Your father is off fighting in the war. Maybe he's dead. You don't know. But suddenly you've had this idea—you can call the operator, and they'll let you talk to him on the phone! Soon, when the operator hangs up on you, you will be very sad, but during the song, you are happy!"

I smiled, but I felt kind of weird about it. The song was really depressing!

And anyway, I couldn't stop thinking about Mr. Gormulka having the calculator. What if Ryan was right about him hunting for a spy in the school? How are you supposed to smile knowing that you could get blown up at any second? I tried to just focus on the music. All spies have to be able to separate their normal lives from their lives as spies, you know. But it wasn't easy.

After "Hello Central," we started working on the next song: a rap that Mr. Cunyan had written himself.

"Now, for this one, you don't need to smile," said Mr. Cunyan as we got started on it. "Because rappers don't smile. You should look either really cool or really tough when you rap. So frown if you want to!"

I didn't know much about rap music, really, but I was pretty sure I knew more about it than Mr. Cunyan. I mean, the guy was about a hundred and fifty! He was probably the least funky person I had ever known in my life.

The rap started out like this:

WHERE ARE THE STUDENTS WHO PEOPLE SAY
ARE THE COOLEST KIDS IN THE USA!
TELL EVERYONE THAT WE'VE PASSED THE TEST—
CORNERSVILLE WEST IS THE VERY BEST!
HOLD ON TIGHT TO THE EDGE OF YOUR SEATS.
OPEN YOUR EYES TO A WHOLE NEW BEAT.
UPON THIS STAGE, WE'RE GOING TO GROOVE—
THIRD GRADERS KNOW HOW TO BUST A MOVE!

See? Even I know a lame rap when I hear one. Plus, I knew that Mr. Cunyan was probably having the kids at Cornersville North, where he taught on Wednesdays and Fridays, say that *they* were the coolest kids in the USA at *their* program. So the rap wasn't even honest. It was just big talk.

"Now, don't forget to count silently to yourself to stay on tempo!" Mr. Cunyan said. He clapped his hands in rhythm to the song and said, "One, two, three, four . . ."

"Hey, Mr. Cunyan," asked Ryan, "did they have that many numbers when you were a kid?"

Mr. Cunyan smiled. Out of all our teachers, he seemed to be the least bothered by Ryan's insults. In fact, he sort of got a kick out of them.

"One through four? Well, sure we did!" said Mr. Cunyan. "We had about twelve numbers back then. The rest of the numbers were discovered when I was in college."

"Wow," Ryan said. "Math must have been easy back then!"

"Nothing was easy back then," said Mr. Cunyan. "I lived on the nineteenth floor in a one-room apartment that we shared with four other families. And there was no elevator, either. We had to walk—upstairs, both ways!"

Mr. Cunyan, in case I didn't mention it, was a very strange person.

When we finished working on the rap, Mr. Cunyan called the three of us who were singing solos on "Kids Are Music" up to the front to practice.

"Kids Are Music," the song I was singing a verse of by myself, was not a very cool song, either. In fact, it was pretty silly. It was all about how kids are full of music from head to toe and how singing makes them want to jump up and down. But I was glad to sing a solo. It was going to give me a chance to wear a suit onstage, and if anyone from the spy company happened to see how sharp I looked in a suit, they'd almost *have* to hire me right on the spot.

If Mr. Gormulka hadn't killed me yet.

I sat patiently through the opening chorus, which the whole class sang, and then through the verse that Madison sang. Could I sneak into Storage Room B after the last bell rang? Maybe I could steal some raw meat from the cafeteria to distract the sharks or construct some sort of suit of armor to protect me against spiders?

But would armor even work against spiders once they caught me in their web?

Maybe I could convince Tony to come along with me and distract the sharks and spiders? It was really more of a job for a monkey. Monkeys were fast and could jump out of the spiders' way, but Tony would probably end up getting eaten.

Suddenly, everything went quiet. The whole class was staring at me. I had been so busy thinking about getting the calculator back that I had missed the cue for my solo!

Mr. Cunyan stopped the recording of the background music. "Andrew," he said, "pay attention, please!"

I blushed. Big time. My face probably went from peach to pink to red and straight into red-violet. You have to be pretty embarrassed to get all the way to red-violet.

"Sorry," I said. "I just got kind of lost, I guess."

"Okay," said Mr. Cunyan. "Let's try this again."

He restarted the music, but this time when I opened my mouth, nothing came out. I froze up!

Mr. Cunyan stopped the recording again. "All right," he said. "I want to try that one more time, okay? I know you can do it, Andrew. You've done it plenty of times before."

I nodded and tried again. That time, I sang it when I was supposed to, but I did a terrible job. I sang all the lines, but I think I got every note wrong. I sounded awful!

"Okay," Mr. Cunyan said as I sat back down on the risers next to Tony. "That was fine."

"No, it wasn't!" said Nicole. "Andrew was really pitchy!"

I gave her a dirty look, but not *too* dirty, because I knew she was right, for once. I had really stunk!

"I'm not worried about that," said Mr. Cunyan. "I know you can do it, Andrew. Are you nervous?"

"Maybe a little," I said. "Not really, though." Good spies *never* admit that they're nervous. It's unprofessional.

"He's just nervous because his brother's calculator is in Storage Room B," said Tony.

I gave his foot a quick kick under the seats.

"I'm sure everything will be fine tomorrow," said Mr. Cunyan. "And even if it isn't, the important thing on this song is that you just keep smiling!"

It honestly hadn't occurred to me that I might screw it up. I had imagined bringing the whole crowd to its feet and maybe having a couple talent scouts offer me a record deal. I hadn't been nervous before, but I was now!

After we finished practicing, Mr. Cunyan gave us a little pep talk.

"Now, I know you guys know these songs very well," he said, "but Mrs. Wellington asked me to tell you how important it is to behave. She wants me to say that anyone who isn't on their best behavior will be in serious trouble. I know you'll all behave, though. I just have to tell you to, anyway, because if there's any trouble, I'll probably be fired. Either that or she'll put me on cafeteria duty for the rest of my life."

"Can you cook?" asked Ryan.

"No," said Mr. Cunyan. "If you have to eat my cooking, you'll all probably die. Of course, if that happens, you'll all get your pictures in the paper for dying in school, and I'll be in there for killing you, so at least we'll all make the news!"

Yep. Mr. Cunyan is a pretty sick person, all right.

Would he really get fired if I messed up my solo? I didn't want to be responsible for something like that! Between worrying about Mr. Cunyan's job and worrying about Mr. Gormulka blowing up the world, I didn't know how I was going to sleep that night.

CHAPTERFIVE

"Number Twenty-seven, you're a genius!" said Andrew "Danger" North as #27, the ultrasecretive weapons designer, showed off his latest creation. To the untrained eye, it looked like an ordinary whistle.

"Give it a try," invited #27.

Agent North pointed the whistle at #29, the agent whose job was to fix the pinball machines at headquarters.

Zzzzzap!

A beam of light shot out at #29 and hit him square on his belt loop. The belt unbuckled itself as if by magic, and #29's pants fell to his feet.

"Works every time!" said #27.

Cheese bags everywhere were going to have to be careful around Agent North now!

When I left school that day, I walked past Storage Room B, which was in the second-grade hall, but Mr. Gormulka was there, whistling while he mopped up the floor outside the room. That creepy kind of whistling.

Since the whole afternoon had gone by and I hadn't heard any explosions, I wondered if maybe Ryan was wrong. Maybe Mr. Gormulka wasn't really a spy; maybe he was just a scary-looking jerk who kept some sort of deep dark secret in Storage Room B. Maybe he wouldn't mess with the calculator. I still had to get it back before Jack found out it was gone, of course, but at least I didn't need to worry about getting blown up. I just had to worry about screwing up the solo.

That's what I told myself, anyway. But all the way home, there was a little voice in the back of my head saying, "What if Ryan's right? What if Mr. Gormulka is just waiting for prime time so he can go on TV and brag about blowing up the world?" If I've learned one thing from all of Dad's spy movies, it's that supervillains usually don't want to blow up the world before they've bragged about it a little. Maybe Mr. Gormulka was just biding his time, waiting for the right opportunity to strike.

As I walked home, I took a shortcut through this little tunnel that went under Tanglewood Parkway. It had a really neat echo when I practiced my solo there. The tunnel was part of a bike path that went up to the pond near the Flowers' Grove neighborhood, but Jack told me that the tunnel was originally built as an escape route during the Civil War. They didn't fight any battles in our state, but that doesn't mean they didn't build escape routes just in case, right?

Jack used to tell me all sorts of secrets like that. There are guys who used to work for the Russians, back when they were the bad guys, living in the Flowers' Grove neighborhood. One of them is our mailman now. And there are dead bodies buried in a house a few houses down from ours, which is on Sanders Street. Jack showed me the exact spot in the backyard where they're buried. I held my breath as I walked past that house, since it's bad luck to go by a cemetery (even a secret one) without holding your breath.

There's weird stuff everywhere in Cornersville Trace. Some of it is pretty obvious, like the statue of the naked angel on a trike at the mall. But most of the weird stuff looks totally normal to people who don't know better. Like Wayne Schneider's house, for instance. It doesn't look like a place where an old rock star who faked his own death would live. It just looks like a regular suburban house. Only people who are in on the secret, like me, would ever suspect that it was anything else.

And my house doesn't look like a spy's house at all. It looks as normal as any other house on the street. I was pretty sure there had to be a pool, a gym, a target range, an obstacle course, a sauna, and all those other things hidden inside someplace—probably deep underground. Spies always have stuff like that in their houses. Besides, that would explain where Jack and Dad really go when they're "at work" or "studying"—they're really working out in our state-of-the-art gym! When I go pro, they'll tell me where the secret passage to get there is. I've looked and looked around the house for it myself, but I haven't found anything.

When I got home, I spent a long time poking around in the cabinets and the basement, trying to find the secret entrance to the underground stuff once and for all. There had to be gadgets in there, some tool I could use to get into Storage Room B and rescue the calculator. But I didn't find a thing.

My mom's not a spy. At least, not anymore. I think maybe she *used* to be, but she gave it all up when Jack was born. She's probably still on the payroll, but now she's a realtor by day. At night, her job is to make our house and family seem as normal as possible. If any bad guys get a clue that Dad or Jack is a spy and try to watch us through the windows, they'll just see a normal family eating casseroles. Mom does a *great* job of making the house seem normal.

But Dad and Jack are still really, really careful not even to talk about spying. Bad guys might have microphones in our walls and telescopes pointed at our windows. That's why I never, ever change clothes with the shades up.

The only time they really talk about spying is when they're watching spy movies. They do it a lot, but I'm hardly ever allowed to watch with them, because Mom thinks they're too violent for me. She makes them wait until I go to bed to turn them on.

But sometimes, when Mom is out late cleaning up a

house she's trying to sell the next day or something, they'll let me watch with them. It's awesome. We just sit around eating popcorn and talking about spy stuff.

I remember one time we were watching an old movie from twenty or thirty years ago, and the spy was using this laser flamethrower thing. It was the size of a vacuum cleaner and was attached to a backpack that he had to wear.

"Ha!" said Dad. "Look at that clunky thing."

"They probably make those things a lot smaller now, huh?" asked Jack.

"Heck, they fit in the palm of your hand now," said Dad. "All the stuff they needed to lug around in backpacks when they made this movie fits on the head of a pin today!"

That's about as close as he ever came to admitting to me that he's a spy. How else would he know how big laser flamethrowers are these days?

I feel like I'm really part of the team on those nights. Most of the time, though, I just have to listen to them hanging out from my bedroom. Then I feel totally left out.

But once I go pro, even Mom will probably let me stay up past nine. And once I'm actually *using* laser flamethrowers, she won't mind letting me watch movies about them.

Jack was having some friends over to play video games that night, so we ate dinner earlier than usual. While we ate our casserole, Mom talked about how hard it was to sell houses that were more than a year old out in the subdivisions west of Eighty-second Street, and Dad talked about how no one was buying insurance that week, either.

Halfway through dinner, Dad turned to me. "Speaking of insurance, guess what, Andrew?" he asked. "My boss is going to be at your music program!"

I couldn't believe it! This was huge! I knew that Dad wasn't *really* an insurance company big shot, so his boss had to be the head of the spy company!

"Oh, really?" I asked, trying to act casual in case any evil spies were listening in.

"Yeppers," said Dad.

He says "yeppers" a lot. It's a good way to keep anyone from ever guessing that he's actually a spy. When people hear him saying dorky things like "yeppers," they'd never dream he's actually a really slick undercover agent. It's actually pretty clever.

"What's he coming for?" I asked.

"He's working on a deal to sell life insurance to Mr. Cunyan, and he thinks showing up to the big night will make a good impression on him."

I knew *that* couldn't be true. See, the idea of life insurance is that the customers pay some money to the insurance company every month, and then when the customers die, the company pays their relatives a bunch of money. But they don't sell insurance to people they think might die before they've made a lot of payments, and Mr. Cunyan looked like he might keel over any minute. No company would sell him life insurance!

Dad's boss was obviously coming to the program to check

me out and see if I was ready to start my official training to be a spy.

Oh God! Maybe I somehow *did* manage to send the message I'd typed into the calculator! The one inviting them to see me at the program. That meant I really had to nail the solo!

Then it got worse.

"Aunt Brianna is coming, too," said Mom.

"Oh, really?" asked Dad. "What's her latest project?"

"I didn't ask," said Mom with a laugh. "I'm sure we'll find out."

"Just as long as she's not trying to sell that weird detergent that made the dishes smell like paste," said Dad.

Aunt Brianna is my mom's little sister. She isn't married yet, and she's never had the same job for more than a couple months. When she came over for Labor Day, she'd decided to become a dancer. By Thanksgiving, she said she'd given that up because she'd found a way to get rich selling cleaning products. She was done with that one by Christmas, though.

"Andrew," Mom said, "you can wear that sweater she made you tomorrow night."

"No, I can't," I said. "I'm wearing my suit."

"That suit you have in your closet must be way too small for you by now," said Mom. "You can't wear that."

"Then let me get another one," I said. "We can go to the store right after dinner!"

"Calm down, Andrew," said Mom. "You don't need to

wear a suit for the program. The sweater will look really cute!"

I gave Dad a sort of desperate look, like, "Come on, you can't really expect me not to wear a suit in front of the head of the spy organization, can you?" but he didn't do a thing. He just kept eating chicken casserole. He sure can be sneaky when he wants to!

I think Dad and Jack try not to tell Mom about any spy stuff. She probably doesn't want to know. The less she knows, the less reason any bad guys have to try to get information out of her. So neither of them would tell her that wearing the sweater Aunt Brianna made on an audition to be a professional spy was a bad, bad idea. And believe me, it was! It made me even *more* nervous. My stomach felt like a pancake that someone was flipping around on a griddle.

See, one thing my mom and Aunt Brianna have in common is that they're both into stuff that's cute. And as cute stuff goes, the sweater Aunt Brianna made me was a real prize. It had a fluffy squirrel on it with cotton balls for a stomach. It would look adorable on a little kid, but it wasn't the sort of thing third graders go around wearing. Especially in front of the head of the spy company!

But the subject was closed. There was no talking my way out of it. Mom and Dad had already changed the subject. They had started nagging Jack instead.

"Remember, Jack, you still have some chores to do," said Mom. "I want you to clean up the living room before your friends get here."

"We're just gonna be in the basement," said Jack. "Who cares what the living room looks like?"

"That's a good point," I said.

"Shut up, Andrew," said Jack.

"Hey!" I said. "I'm on your side!"

I hate to say this, but sometimes I really hate Jack's guts. Sometimes to cover up the fact that he's a spy, he has to act like a real jerk. He's hardly paid a bit of attention to me since he turned thirteen. I knew it was because he was busy with spy stuff, but it still stank. I missed hanging out with him.

"Just clean up the living room, Jack," said Dad. "What're you guys going to be doing?"

"Nothing much," said Jack. "We'll probably just listen to music and play Blood Suckers Three."

Dad raised an eyebrow.

"It's a video game," I said. "You have to kill vampires in it."

Dad nodded. "Yeppers," he said thoughtfully. "You've got to watch out for those vampires. They'll suck the blood right out of you."

"Hence the name Blood Suckers," said Jack impatiently.

"That's what they do, all right," said Mom. "They'll suck your brains out like they were eating snail out of a shell!"

And she and Dad started making slurping noises and laughing. Jack looked up at the ceiling and sighed. A minute later, he cleared his plate and disappeared up to his room.

"He sure eats fast these days," I said, hoping maybe they'd let it slip that he had to eat quickly so he could get back to work on saving the world. I knew it was almost definitely true that Dad and Jack were spies, but I really wished they'd admit it just once so I'd know for sure.

"He's a teenager now," said Mom with a sigh. "He'll start eating us out of house and home soon."

"And don't forget this one," said Dad, pointing at me. "Four years from now, we're going to have *two* teenagers in the house."

"Don't remind me," said Mom.

"Well, sor-ry!" I said. "It's not *my* fault I'll be a teenager soon!"

Parents are always doing that—acting like it's *not* their fault their kids were born or something!

A few minutes later, just before Jack's friends showed up, Jack came back downstairs.

"Have you guys seen my calculator?" he asked. "I can't find it in my room."

I gulped.

"Gee, Jack," said Mom sarcastically. "How in the world could anything get lost in your clean, clean room?"

Jack sighed. "Just keep an eye out for it, will you?" he asked. "I'm really going to need it this weekend."

"Do you need it right now?" I asked.

Jack shrugged. "Not really," he said.

"Do you need it tomorrow?" I asked.

Jack shrugged again. "I'm not really going to need it un-til this weekend. Why? Have you seen it?"

"No," I said. "Just curious."

"You better not have taken it!" said Jack.

"He wouldn't do that, Jack," said Mom. "Andrew knows not to mess with your stuff."

"Yeah!" I said. "Maybe you left it at school or something."

"I hope so," said Jack. "If I don't have that thing back by the weekend, I'm dead. Really, really dead."

Gulp. Jack must need it for some really important mission over the weekend!

Even if Mr. Gormulka *didn't* use the calculator to blow something up, the fate of the world depended on whether I could get it back the next day!

CHAPTER SIX

London. Midnight has come and gone. The DJ sits in his booth at the trendiest nightclub in the United Kingdom.

Fog everywhere. Fog on the club's dance floor, mingling with the dancers, who jostle one another, pretending not to be blinded by the strobe lights. Fog flowing into the VIP room, shrouding the face of the young man with the excellent suit and perfect hair.

No one on the dance floor knows that the club is owned by Dr. Cringe, who is secretly testing a strange new drug on the dancers. Anyone who orders a cranberry juice from the bar will find—too late—that their drink has been spiked with a strange potion that will cause them to cluck like a chicken for several hours. If he can perfect the drug and introduce it into the world's water supply, Dr. Cringe will turn all of humanity into a bunch of clucking idiots!

Back in his disguise as Thaddeus Arthur III, heir to the Arthur Badminton Equipment fortune, Agent North does his best to look tired, bored, and cranky, like everyone else in the nightclub. He has been trained to fit into any group.

Then, one of the dancers, the tiredest and crankiest of them all, looks at Andrew.

"Hey, kid!" he says. "Get out of here! Didn't Mom ask you to take the garbage out?"

An hour later, Jack and his friends Jason and Todd were downstairs, playing video games—something he used to do with *me* before he turned thirteen. I could understand why he couldn't tell me spy secrets now that he'd gone pro, but I was pretty annoyed that he wasn't even playing games with me anymore, since he was obviously still allowed to play them with his friends. *They* weren't all pro spies. They couldn't be!

I could tell they were having a pretty good time down there, but I didn't want to interrupt. Instead, I just sat down at the piano and tried to figure out how to play "Kids Are Music." After a while, I'd managed to pick out the melody pretty well. I had never had any piano lessons, either! I'll bet if I had one or two, they'd say I was a musical genius.

"That's such a happy song," said Mom when she heard me playing. "Jack had to sing it one year, too. And now listen to the stuff he likes! That music they're playing down there is depressing."

"So is one of the other songs we're singing," I said. "It's a really sad old parlor song."

"Yeah," said Mom. "There's always one really depressing song in the program, isn't there? When Jack was in third grade, he had to sing some old song about a girl whose brother dies waiting for their dad to come home from a bar!"

"Sounds like the stuff Mr. Cunyan likes," I said.

"It still can't be as bad as that music Jack likes," said Mom. "There's not a happy song in his whole collection."

"Mr. Cunyan's stuff is worse," I said. "Believe me."

"I doubt it," said Mom. "Go down there in the basement and listen to whatever they're playing on the stereo. I'll bet you a dollar to a donut it's more depressing than what you're singing tomorrow!"

I sighed. "I don't think Jack wants me down there with all his friends."

"Yeah?" said Mom. "Well, Jack doesn't have a choice. I bought the Mountain Dew they're drinking, so if I say you can be down there, you can be down there. Go ahead."

This sounded like an order. And of course I wanted to go down there; they sounded like they were having fun. Being ordered to was as good an excuse as any. I got up and headed to the basement door.

I know I was just going down to the basement, but it felt like I was going into the danger zone. Jack was down there, probably all ready to be a jerk. And Todd was in high school. High school! High schoolers aren't always known to be very nice to third graders.

So I decided to keep a low profile, almost like spying. I opened the door to the basement really slowly so it didn't make a single creak, and I walked down really slowly, without making a sound. I was pretty successful, if I do say so myself. Jack had taught me well. I'd been down there a couple of minutes, just watching them play video games, before he even noticed I was there.

"Get lost, kid," he told me with a sneer.

"Mom sent me down here to listen to the music," I said. "She thinks it's depressing."

Todd turned to me and made what I guess he thought was a scary face.

"It's evil music," he said in a low, creepy voice. "It's all about demons! It'll make you want to kill your parents!"

I shrugged, trying to act cool. "It still can't be as bad as the stuff Mr. Cunyan likes," I said.

"Oh man!" groaned Todd. "Mr. Cunyan? That guy's not dead yet?"

"Man," said Jason. "That guy was a wacko!"

"Is he making you sing a parlor song at the program this year?" asked Todd.

I nodded.

"Remember when we had to sing 'Down on the Farm'?" said Jason. And he started singing, "How ya gonna keep them down on the farm, after they've seen Paree?"

Then Todd sang, "How you gonna keep them down on the farm after they've seen you pee?" and everyone laughed.

"What about 'The Pennsylvania Polka'?" asked Jason. And he started singing that one, too. "It started in Scranton; it's now number one . . . the Pennsylvania Polka!"

"Man," said Todd, "high school sucks, but at least nobody makes me sing old geezer music anymore."

"The program is tomorrow night," I said. "It's gonna stink, too. All the songs are lame. And I have to sing a solo."

"You poor kid," said Todd. "If I had to do that, I'd just go hide somewhere they'd never find me."

"Like Storage Room B?" I asked. I figured that while I

had them talking, I'd see if *they* knew anything. It was some awfully good spying, if I do say so myself.

"Yeah!" said Todd. "Man, I know a kid who spent his whole life trying to get into that room. No one gets in there. Not even teachers!"

"It's probably where Mr. Gormulka keeps all his stuff," said Jason. "Is that guy still around, too?"

"Yeah," I said. "They say he guards that room with his life."

"Well, sure he does," said Todd. "Everyone knows Gormulka's stashing anything valuable that ever got lost in that room, anyway. I heard there's some huge collection of comic books in there. He's probably gonna sell it off when he retires and use the money to move to Florida."

"Mark Brueggen once told me he had a secret spy head-quarters in there," said Jason.

"Mark Brueggen is a dork," said Jack, rolling his eyes.

Jack and his friends started ignoring me and talking about everyone else they knew who was a dork besides Mark Brueggen, but at least no one was telling me to get lost. It looked like as long as I stayed out of the way and didn't run up to tell Mom that they were swearing, I was okay. I even made a point of swearing along with them when someone got killed in the video game, just so they knew that I wasn't some little kid who didn't know how to swear.

I had been hoping one of them would tell me that Storage Room B was just a little closet full of old mittens and that there was an easy way to pick the lock, but no such luck. It looked like I was in just as much trouble as I thought I was!

I didn't think they really knew much, though. Maybe Todd and Jason were their class's version of Tony Zunker—people told them weird stuff just to see if they believed it, and they did!

But it was interesting that they'd both heard about the comic books being in there. A lot of people seemed to think that. It almost had to be true! If I got in there, maybe I could look through them a bit. A long time ago, I saw an ad in an old comic book offering pet monkeys for only $19.95, but I stupidly didn't write the address down. The comic book was about forty years old, but I'll bet I could still send money to that address. There's no way they could go out of business offering a deal as great as that.

When I'd been down in the basement for about fifteen minutes, Mom came down with a load of laundry to toss in the washing machine.

"Are they giving you any trouble, Andrew?" asked Mom.

I shrugged. "Nah," I said.

"Are they letting you play?" she asked.

"Yeah," I said. "I played a lot."

I hadn't actually played at all, of course. I hadn't even asked to. But I knew that if I said no, Mom would give Jack a talking-to right there, and he'd never forgive me for it.

"Good," she said.

I noticed that Jack even gave me a tiny little thanks-for-not-getting-me-in-trouble nod at that point. And after Mom left, he didn't even try to stop me from grabbing a can of Mountain Dew.

I had successfully infiltrated the group. That's what spies call it when they break into a group and don't get kicked out or discovered: infiltrating it. I sat back, sipped a Mountain Dew, and swore right along with them. It was awesome. It was like getting to be a teenager four years early!

After everyone had gone home, I started thinking up plans to get the calculator/communicator back.

I just needed to distract Mr. Gormulka. Maybe I could just eat some of the potato salad and puke it back up. Then, while Mr. Gormulka was busy cleaning up the puke, I'd escape from the nurse's office, pick the lock to Storage Room B, and get the calculator back. Just like that!

But I didn't kid myself: that plan wasn't exactly foolproof. For one thing, eating the potato salad might not really make me puke. Other people ate it on Fridays, and they seemed to do okay. For another, if it *did* make me puke, it might make me too sick to escape from the nurse's office in the first place. And what if I couldn't get the lock picked? I still didn't really have a plan for that.

I was just working on a plan B when Jack came into my room.

"Hey, man," Jack said.

"Hey!" I said. I could hardly believe it. Jack hadn't come into my room in months! Maybe he wanted to compliment me on my swearing.

"You wanna know the truth about Mr. Gormulka?" he asked. "It's top-secret, but I think you should know."

"Sure!" I said, sitting upright. Jack hadn't told me any secrets about the town in months!

"That Mark Brueggen kid is a dork, but he's also right," said Jack. "Gormulka's a spy. For the bad guys. He works at the school because he knows there are spies here in Cornersville Trace, and being a janitor makes it easy for him to spy on kids."

I couldn't believe it. Ryan Kowalski had been telling the truth!

"So why don't the good guys arrest him?" I asked.

"He's way too clever for that," said Jack. "There's no real evidence that will hold up in court against him. Everyone at the spy headquarters knows he's a spy, but no one can prove it. You can't just arrest people and send them to jail without proof!"

"So you've been to headquarters, then?" I asked, hoping that he'd finally admit it.

"No comment," said Jack. "I shouldn't be telling you all this. It's top-secret stuff. But I have to warn you that you could be in big trouble."

"Really?" I asked.

"I think Gormulka is zeroing in on someone at the school," said Jack. "And it's probably you. And the last time he attacked a student, it was during the music program."

"No way!" I said.

"Seriously," said Jack. He lowered his voice to almost a

whisper and leaned in close to me. "It was when we sang 'The Pennsylvania Polka.' There was a kid in my class that year named Will Hannon who was always trying to break into Storage Room B. When I look back on it now, I'm sure that he was a spy. He told me he'd seen a bunch of comic books in there when he walked past while Mr. Gormulka was opening the door. On the day of the program, he told me he'd finally gotten inside and that he'd be telling me what was in there soon. But right before we went onstage, he disappeared. And he was supposed to be singing a solo, just like you're doing tomorrow!"

"He just disappeared?" I asked as a chill ran down my spine.

"They never saw him again," said Jack. "The school tried to cover it up. They said that he'd never shown up for the program at all and that his family had moved to Florida. But I know he was there that night . . . and then he was gone."

"You think Mr. Gormulka got him?" I asked.

"Of course," said Jack. "His family had to go into hiding so Mr. Gormulka couldn't get the rest of them, too. I don't know if he's still alive or not. All I know is that when we were singing 'The Pennsylvania Polka,' I thought I heard him screaming out in the hall. No one in the auditorium noticed, because we were drowning out the screams with our singing!"

"Wow," I said quietly. My knees were shaking. For a second there, I noticed Jack looked like he was almost smiling. I guess he was trying not to get me *too* scared.

"So I just wanted to warn you to be careful tomorrow

night," said Jack. "Watch out for Mr. Gormulka, and don't try to take him on yourself! Even the best spies at headquarters think he's too dangerous to fight!"

"What do you think he's hiding in Storage Room B?" I asked.

"I have no idea," said Jack. "Those comic books are probably just bait to lure spies into the place. Who knows what he's really hiding? I want you to promise me you won't try to get into that room, no matter what."

I paused for a second. "What if I knew that something was in there?" I asked. "Something really important?"

"Forget it!" said Jack. "It's not important enough to get killed over! Got it?"

I nodded. Jack nodded back, shook my hand, and then went back to his room without another word.

I had always known that Mr. Gormulka was kind of a jerk, but it was crazy that he was really *that* dangerous!

I had promised Jack I wouldn't go in there, but now I knew I had to do it. I had no choice. A dangerous guy like Mr. Gormulka could use that calculator to take over the world if I didn't get it back!

CHAPTER**SEVEN**

Agent North felt the cool metal of the chains chafing his wrists as he dangled above the shark tank.

"It's curtains for you, North!" shouted Dr. Cringe. As North was lowered closer and closer to the water, Dr. Cringe raised a mop in the air and laughed in triumph, then began whistling "The Pennsylvania Polka."

North fell closer and closer, kicking his legs, trying to block out the incredibly creepy sound and hoping and praying that Dave the Monkey would show up and rescue him. . . .

I was tired the next morning, because every time I nearly got to sleep the night before, I'd imagine getting eaten by a shark in a secret shark tank under the school. Or sometimes I just imagined Mr. Gormulka turning the calculator in to his bosses, who used information from it to capture Jack and my dad and hold them hostage in some secret chamber under the South Pole guarded by penguins with chips in their brains that turned them into evil kung fu experts. If they got captured—or worse—it would be all my fault. I barely got two hours of sleep the whole night!

What if Mr. Gormulka kidnapped me in the middle of the program, like he did to Will Hannon? What if he realized that I was from a family of spies, and used the calculator to blow up the whole auditorium and get rid of my whole family, including Aunt Brianna, at once? Sure, he'd take out the entire auditorium, too, but supervillains don't care much about innocent bystanders. He'd probably be happy about it!

Even if my whole family *didn't* get blown up, I still had to worry about nailing my solo. I was still kind of afraid I was going to mess up—while wearing a cutesy sweater in front of the head of the spy company!

Mom made me a special breakfast with eggs and pancakes instead of regular old cereal, but I could hardly eat. I was so nervous, I thought I might puke.

Just before we left for school, Jack turned to me and whispered, "Remember what I told you. Stay away from Mr. Gormulka!"

"I will," I said.

But I knew I had to get that calculator back.

All through math class that morning, I kept my eye out for Mr. Gormulka. It's scary to be trapped in school when you know someone there is out to get you! Whenever I heard a door open or heard the sound of someone dropping a book, I jumped about a foot in the air.

In the morning, I said I had to go to the bathroom and tried to sneak into Storage Room B while I knew Mr. Gormulka would be setting up tables in the lunchroom, but Mrs. Rademacher was in the hall, prowling around. There was no getting past her.

I was so caught up worrying about getting into that room that I almost forgot to be nervous about the music program until right after recess, when Mrs. Wellington, the principal, came into the room. She just walked right in without knocking. Principals don't have to knock.

"Hi, Joyce," said Mr. Summers.

"Hello, Brian!" she said cheerfully. "I need to borrow your class for a minute, please."

Mr. Summers nodded and motioned her in. Teachers always have to do what the principal wants.

"Hi, boys and girls!" said Mrs. Wellington. "How's everyone feeling today?"

"Better than you look!" said Ryan Kowalski. A few kids giggled. Even Mrs. Wellington smiled a little. But she always smiled. I've almost never seen her not smiling.

"That's good," she said. "Might as well get it out of your system now, Ryan. I just came by to remind all of you to be on your very best behavior tonight at the music program. You will be, won't you?"

Everyone nodded. Why wouldn't they nod? I mean, if some kid was planning to throw a water balloon in the middle of it, they wouldn't blurt that out to Mrs. Wellington, would they? No one was *that* stupid.

"Wonderful!" she said. "I also just want to remind everyone to dress up *really nicely* tonight for the *big show*! When your parents and grandparents and aunts and uncles see you up there, *smiling* and singing those *great* songs, they're just going to feel *so good* inside!"

She hugged herself to show us how good our parents were going to feel.

"You mean like this?" asked Ryan. And he smiled a *really* big smile, the kind that normal people don't go around making because it hurts their face.

"Just like that!" said Mrs. Wellington. "That's exactly what I mean. *Super* job, Ryan!"

"Okay," said Ryan. "But I'm gonna need a couple of Popsicle sticks and a fishhook, and I'll be sore in the morning!"

"Whatever you have to do," said Mrs. Wellington. And she winked. She did that a lot. Every time I passed Mrs. Wellington in the hall, she winked at me, like I was sharing a secret with her or something.

I used to wonder if she was winking to tell me she knew all about my dad's secret job, but I eventually figured out that she was just really into winking at people. Some people are nuts about math, and some are nuts about winking. Normally I would say that Mr. Summers was probably better off, since being able to do math is way more important than winking, but she was *his* boss. The world's a weird place sometimes.

"Now, those of you who are singing solos, make sure you smile and do your best!" said Mrs. Wellington. She looked right at me, Nicole, and Madison, since each of us was singing a verse of the song "Kids Are Music."

"We will," Nicole said, quietly enough that I could hear her but Mrs. Wellington couldn't. "If Andrew doesn't mess up."

I glared at her.

"I'm sure they'll all be fine, Joyce," said Mr. Summers.

"Of course they will!" said Mrs. Wellington. "The program is going to be *super*! Right, gang?"

Everyone nodded again.

"Great!" she said. "Remember: big smiles!"

And she walked out to give the same speech to the next class.

"You can stop smiling now, Ryan," said Mr. Summers. "We can all get back to work."

"You know why she wants us to smile like idiots, right?" Ryan asked. "It's so our parents start to worry that we *are* idiots! If they think we're growing up stupid, they'll donate more money to the school to make us smarter!"

"That's enough, Ryan," said Mr. Summers, though I could see he was trying not to laugh.

I thought Ryan was on to something. Jack once told me

that Mrs. Wellington got so pumped up about the music program because it was the best chance she had all year to hit our parents up for money.

That afternoon we had gym class, which I figured was good for me. It would give me a chance to get some exercise and maybe build up my strength a bit. I was going to need it!

Weirdly enough, our gym teacher, Coach Walker, is an old lady who isn't even in very good shape. She's always bent over like her back is hurting, and she's always walking around muttering "Oh, my lungs and liver!" like she's in really terrible pain. I think maybe they just let her be the gym teacher so we can see how we'll end up if we don't exercise.

Some people think Coach Walker and Mr. Cunyan are secretly married. They're about the same age, after all. I asked Jack about that once, and even he thought it was possible. He didn't know for sure, though. It's a mystery.

"All right, children," said Coach Walker as we all walked into the gym. She never shouted at us, like some gym teachers do—she didn't have the voice for it. Every time she tried to shout, it came out more like a croak. "I know tonight is your music program, so I am not going to work you very hard today."

Everyone cheered.

"Today you are going to play Impossible Mission!"

Everyone cheered again, especially me. Impossible Mission is the most fun game ever invented by a gym teacher.

It's a game where you have to use your head. It was a perfect way to warm up for a spy mission!

Coach Walker went to her supply closet, and a couple kids started helping her pull out jump ropes, crates, brooms, little scooters, and junk like that. The idea of Impossible Mission is that she divides us up into teams, and each team has to get every member of the team from one end of the gym to the other using all the junk from the closet. The trick is that you're not allowed to touch the floor. You have to use the jump ropes and stuff to get across without touching the ground. It's pretty awesome. And I'm great at it! If there was an Impossible Mission team at the high school, I could totally make the varsity squad.

She divided all the junk into four piles and divided us into teams. I was hoping she would put me on Tony's team, but no such luck. I was stuck in a group with Neil, Matt, and Melvin Purvis. Melvin Purvis might be an even bigger geek than poor Tony. With a name like that, he sort of has to be. He's really rich, though, so no one picks on him. Every time someone does, he threatens to have his dad sue them.

"All right," said Coach Walker. "You may begin . . . now!"

"Okay, guys," I said to my team. "If you just wanna sit back, I can get us through this."

"Shut up!" said Neil.

"Yeah, Andrew," said Matt. "You stink at this game!"

"No, I don't!" I insisted. "I'm practically a professional!"

"A professional?" Neil sneered. "You can't be a professional Impossible Mission player. I'm in charge of this team, and that's final!"

"Let's vote on it," I said. "All in favor of Neil being in charge?"

"Aye!" said Neil and Matt.

"And all in favor of me?" I asked, raising my own hand. I looked over at Melvin. "Come on, Purvis!" I said. "Are you gonna vote or not?"

Melvin shook his head. "I'm not voting for anyone," he said. "I don't want to be too involved."

"Why not?" I asked.

"If I get involved and someone gets hurt, it could be my fault," he said. "I don't want to get sued!"

What a dork!

"That settles it, then!" said Neil. "I'm in charge."

"Fine," I said. "But let's get started, all right? We're already behind, and I don't wanna lose!"

I already had a whole bunch of ideas for how to get across the gym without touching the ground. We could put the crate on top of the little scooter thing and push the first person across the floor. Then that person would hop off, push the scooter back, and get everyone else across on it. We could use the jump rope as a tow rope and pull the last person across. It was simple.

"All right," said Neil. "I'll go across first."

He stepped into the milk crate and started slowly

wiggling it. He was moving forward, but it would take him all day to get across, and he'd never be able to get it back across the floor to us once he got there.

"Come on, Neil!" I said. "That's never going to work."

"Shut your face, An-dy!"

I felt all the blood in my body rush up into my eyes. It probably turned my pupils bright red and made them look all scary and everything.

"*Shut up!*" I shouted.

Just then, I felt a hand on my shoulder. It was Coach Walker.

"What did you just say, Andrew?" she croaked.

"I was just doing some trash talk," I said, real casual-like. "You know. Like people do in sports."

"Do not give me any of that, Andrew," said Coach Walker. "Being a poor sport is not the way to play, and I will not tolerate language like that in my gymnasium. Come with me!"

She grabbed my shoulder and led me away from the gym. Coach Walker thinks a lot of words that most people say all the time are curse words. Words like "butt" and "fart." I guess people thought those were curse words when she was a kid, about a hundred years ago.

"What's going to happen to my team if I don't get to play?" I asked, as if I even cared.

"Never mind that," she said. "Instead of playing with the rest of the class, you're going to help Mr. Gormulka today."

I felt a chill through my entire body.

"No!" I said. "Please! Can't I just go clean all the bathrooms or something? I'll do a good job!"

"Nonsense," said Coach Walker. "Mr. Gormulka is right down the hall. You can help him with his duties."

Coach Walker led me out into the third-grade hall. I followed along but pretty slowly, seeing as I was almost positive I was about to get dunked in a shark tank or attacked by evil penguins or something. Mr. Gormulka was wiping down lockers. When he saw me coming, he glared at me and raised his eyebrows. His scar went up right along with them. My knees began to shake.

"I have a helper for you today, Mr. Gormulka," said Coach Walker.

"What's he in trouble for?" asked Mr. Gormulka.

"Foul language," said Coach Walker. "He will be with you the rest of the gym period."

Mr. Gormulka nodded, and Coach Walker walked away. I shivered, waiting to be dragged off to Storage Room B. But Mr. Gormulka just handed me a rag.

"Wipe," he said, pointing at the lockers.

I just stood there for a second. I was almost too scared to move. He must have looked at the calculator and figured out that I was a spy. So why was he letting me live? Maybe he was going to work me to death or something! He'd make me wipe down hundreds and hundreds of lockers until I died of exhaustion!

"Don't just stand there, North," he said. "Get to work."

I sighed and started wiping down lockers slowly, to keep my strength up. After I got through three or four of them, I started to think maybe he wasn't going to kill me right then. Maybe he hadn't figured out the truth about the calculator yet, or maybe he was waiting to kill me during the program. Either way, I was probably safe for now, but I kept my eye on him. I wasn't going to let him sneak up on me and attack!

While we worked, Mr. Gormulka whistled. It was a pretty happy tune, but it still sounded super creepy to me.

I started on locker #27, and I was up to locker #41 when Mr. Gormulka suddenly got a call on his walkie-talkie.

"We have a two-thirteen in first-grade hall!" said a voice.

"Oh geez!" said Mr. Gormulka. And he ran off down the hall, shouting, "Keep working" over his shoulder. He was in such a hurry that he didn't even bother to pick up all his tools. He just left his tool belt lying on the floor.

I wondered what a 213 was. Probably something pretty nasty, like someone puking. Or maybe it wasn't anything to do with cleaning at all; maybe it meant that the head of his organization was calling him on the video phone in his secret hideout, and he had to go talk to him! Maybe he was getting instructions to make me "disappear" right then!

I kept on working for a second, but then I turned to look at his tool belt sitting on the floor. What if there was a murder weapon or a secret gadget or something on there? If I could be the person who finally found proof they could use to arrest Mr. Gormulka, spy headquarters would almost *have* to hire me on the spot!

I walked over to the tool belt and picked it up. At first I was disappointed. It looked like just a regular bunch of tools, without any bloodstains on them or anything. But then I saw something shiny poking out of a little pocket. A ring of keys! I looked closer and saw that there was a label on one of them that said STORAGE ROOM B—COPY.

Oh man! A key to Storage Room B!

This was my big chance! I could get into Storage Room B while Mr. Gormulka was busy with the 213—whatever that was—get the calculator, and get back to wiping lockers before he even knew I was gone. The only thing I had to worry about was that he might be in Storage Room B himself, taking a call on the video phone. After all, if Mr. Gormulka had a secret spy video phone, it had to be in Storage Room B. But it was a risk I had to take.

I could handle it.

I was Andrew "Danger" North!

I took the key off the ring and put it in my pocket, took a deep breath, and started walking down the second-grade hall. When I got to Storage Room B, I reached into my pocket and fished out the key.

This was *it*! I was acting like a real spy now, breaking into the secret hideout of Mr. Gormulka. And without any gadgets or monkeys to help me. I only hoped the booby traps wouldn't kill me.

I was just about to put the key into the keyhole when I heard a shout from down the hall: *"Freeze!"*

I gulped. It was Mr. Gormulka! And when I turned

around, I saw him staring down at me, just a few feet away now, with a killer's look in his eye!

I thought about making a run for it, but he was too close to me. My heart was beating so loud I could barely think, but I knew I was going to have to *talk* my way out of this one.

"What in the world do you think you're doing?" he barked.

"Um, nothing," I said as I shoved the key back in my pocket before he could see it. (That wasn't a brilliant start, I knew, but it bought me some time.) "I was just looking for you to tell you how I was doing on the lockers." *Genius!*

"Don't try to talk your way out of this, North," said Mr. Gormulka. "Believe me, I know a liar when I see one! You were trying to get into this storage room!"

"No I wasn't!" I said.

"This room is off-limits!" he said, so forcefully that he was spitting a little. *Yuck.* "No one gets into this room. No one! Not even teachers! If I ever catch you poking around here again, you'll be in more trouble than you could ever imagine. Understand?"

I nodded.

"Good," he said. "Now go finish wiping down those lockers!"

Was it possible he *still* wasn't going to kill me? Even after he'd caught me trying to sneak into his secret lair?

He must have something truly dastardly planned for the concert.

I got back to wiping down the lockers, and eventually

Mr. Gormulka came back. He scowled at me while I worked, but he still didn't try to kill me. He just went back to wiping down lockers and doing that awful whistling.

Just before the class came out of the gym and started heading back to the classroom, I recognized the melody Mr. Gormulka was whistling. It was the song that Jason had sung a bit of in the basement the day before: "The Pennsylvania Polka"! The song that the class had been singing while Mr. Gormulka killed Will Hannon!

My knees started shaking. For whatever reason, Mr. Gormulka had decided to let me live for now—even after finding me in front of his secret lair.

But he was obviously planning to kill me that night at the music program!

CHAPTEREIGHT

Agent North had had to wear some ridiculous disguises on his spy missions. There was the time in Chicago when he had to disguise himself as a garbageman, complete with garbage stuck to his face. There was the night in Africa when he had to dress up as the back end of a camel. And, of course, there was the time in Switzerland when he had to dress up like that girl from the instant-hot-chocolate box. It was all part of the job.

But as North pulled on the sweater with the fluffy squirrel on it, he considered turning in his resignation. If he had to dress up like this to keep Dr. Cringe from stealing the Liberty Bell, well, then Dr. Cringe could just go ahead and steal it! It was only a bell, after all. And it was already broken, anyway!

"I have been reborn!" said Aunt Brianna. We were all at the table, eating an early dinner before the program.

That might sound like a big deal, but really it wasn't. Aunt Brianna gets "reborn" all the time. It's what she says every time she gets a new hobby or "career path." When I was in first grade, she was "reborn" as a vegetarian, and for a while there it seemed like she wouldn't even eat lettuce if she thought the truck that brought it to the store might have frightened a cow on the way. But then the next time we saw her, she had been reborn again, and now she was into Italian cooking, which involved a lot of meat.

"What is it this time?" Mom asked.

"I'm going to become an alpaca farmer!" she announced.

"What's an alpaca?" I asked.

"They're sort of like llamas, only they don't bite," said Aunt Brianna. "They're the cutest creatures you ever saw in your life."

"Cuter than monkeys?" I asked.

"By far!" said Aunt Brianna.

I didn't argue with her, but it's a well-known fact that no animal in the world is cuter than a monkey. Some people might say dolphins are cuter, but those people are wrong.

"So, how does one go about becoming an alpaca farmer, Bri?" asked Mom.

I could see she was just humoring her, like people humor four-year-olds who say they're building a rocket ship. Aunt Brianna didn't seem to notice.

"Well, it doesn't cost that much to get started," she said.

"Less than I paid for my car. I'm going to buy two alpacas and rent space at a farm for them until they start breeding. After that, I'll be making so much money selling the wool that I can buy my own land and start up my own farm next year! There's an empty space up north of Preston that I can probably get really cheap."

"Well, of course it's cheap," said Dad. "It's in the middle of nowhere."

"It won't be for long," said Mom. "That land would be a bargain."

"Yeah," said Aunt Brianna. "It's a really good investment. Once they build that giant new mall in Preston, the whole area's going to explode, and the price of the land will go way up. Then I'll sell it at a huge profit and buy a cheap farm somewhere else. So I'll be making money from the land *and* the wool!"

"How much does the wool go for?" asked Dad.

"Lots," said Aunt Brianna. "It's the best wool in the world. And I can use plenty of it for my own knitting, of course, so you guys can count on getting some pretty fantastic sweaters!"

I forced myself to smile, but it wasn't easy.

I was wearing the sweater that she'd given me. I looked like such a dork that I wanted to punch *myself*. There was no way that people like Neil would be able to resist making fun of me. I wished I had an extra five bucks to buy some really choice insults before the program, but it was looking like I'd just have to think on my feet.

Fortunately, that's something spies are really good at.

"Well, I sure hope you'll invite us out to see the alpacas," said Mom. Then she turned to me. "Andrew," she said, "what are you going to be singing tonight besides your solo?"

"We're doing three songs," I said. "Besides the one I'm doing, there's that parlor song I told you about and then a rap song."

"Mr. Cunyan is teaching you to rap?" asked Jack. "That's gotta be lame!"

"I think it's fantastic," said Aunt Brianna. "He must be very open to multiculturalism to introduce you suburban kids to urban music."

"Everyone already knows about rap," I said. "I think we all know more about it than Mr. Cunyan does. He mostly likes old-fashioned songs about people dying and stuff."

"I can't believe that guy is even still alive!" said Jack.

"Maybe he isn't," I said. "Maybe he's a zombie!"

"Be nice!" said Mom. "I think it's wonderful that a man of his age is willing to explore modern musical styles. Which rap song are you singing, Andrew?"

"One that Mr. Cunyan wrote," I said.

Jack was laughing. "*Mr. Cunyan* wrote a *rap* song? I'd die before I sang a rap song that guy wrote in front of people!"

"Jack!" said Mom. "That's not very polite."

"I don't blame him, Mom," I said. "I might very well die tonight because of it. I'll die of embarrassment!" I tried to point down at the sweater sneakily so that Mom would notice but Aunt Brianna wouldn't. Mom, Dad, and Jack got the message. Jack started laughing even harder.

"I almost wish I was going now," said Jack between chuckles. "Just to see that!"

"You *are* going," Mom said.

Jack stopped laughing. "What do you mean?" he asked.

"I mean you're going to the program," said Mom. "What made you think you weren't going?"

"I just thought that maybe I could just, you know, hang out at home," said Jack. "You know they can always use an extra seat."

"Jack!" said Mom. "It's your brother's music program. Of course you're going. He went to all of yours before he was even in school."

"Oh, it's all right," I said. "He doesn't have to."

I really wanted Jack to go back to thinking I was cool, like he used to. And I didn't think that was going to be possible if he saw me rapping in a cutesy-wootsy sweater. Besides, if I was able to successfully fend off Neil's insults, foil Mr. Gormulka's evil plot to kill us all, get Jack's calculator back from Storage Room B, and nail my solo—a pretty tall order for a normal kid but not for a superspy like myself—then the next time Jack saw me, Dad's boss would have called me up for training, just like him. Then we could work together to save the world from evil spies like Mr. Gormulka, just like we used to.

"Of course he has to," said Mom. "There's no question about it."

Jack sighed, got up, and walked to his room without even glancing in my direction. I felt my heart sink a little. I'd tried to help him, and he hadn't even noticed. Now he was probably going to be a big jerk all through the whole music program. Mom followed him, probably to give him a lecture.

I stared down at my food, trying not to let it show that I was upset. And kind of scared. And kind of worried that my complete failure to get into Storage Room B when I had a chance meant that I might not be cut out for spy training after all.

"You okay, Andrew?" asked Dad.

I nodded and didn't look at him or Aunt Brianna. I knew that it was one of those times when if I opened my mouth at all, I'd start crying.

"Come on, champ," said Aunt Brianna, who hadn't figured out that no one over the age of five likes to be called "champ." "What's wrong?"

"Nothing," I muttered.

"Jack's going through a tough age," Dad told me. "Some people say that being a teenager is the best time of your life, but they don't remember how hard it is to be thirteen."

"Jeez," said Aunt Brianna. "That was the worst year of my life."

"Don't take it personally," said Dad. "He's being a real jerk to your mom and me these days, too. And it hurts our feelings, too, even though we always knew he'd be like this when he was thirteen. Almost everyone is like that when they're thirteen. You probably will be, too."

I nodded, but I didn't feel much better, if you want to know the truth. I knew Mrs. Wellington was going to be upset with me, but I didn't think I could smile very much at the program.

A few minutes later, we all piled into the car. Jack had come out of his bedroom, but he still wore an angry scowl, like he was too cool for this. Aunt Brianna sat in the back, next to me and Jack. While she and my parents had a chat about alpacas and real estate, Jack leaned over to me.

"You all set?" he asked, quietly enough that the adults wouldn't notice.

I was surprised that he was talking to me at all. "Sure," I said.

"Just be careful," he said. "You know why."

Jack was trying to warn me! I guess he did care what happened to me at the music program after all. "I will," I said, dropping my voice to a whisper. "Listen, I'm a little worried that if Mr. Gormulka had a gadget that could blow up the whole school, he'd probably pick tonight to use it, wouldn't he? Since Dad's boss is going to be there?"

Jack nodded gravely. "Absolutely," he said. "No doubt about it. He wouldn't care how many regular people he had to blow up if he could get me, Dad, *and* the head of the company. That's a bunch of very important spies right there. I wouldn't worry, though. From the intelligence we got this week, it doesn't sound like he has any gadgets that could do that."

I felt like I'd just eaten about six helpings of Friday potato salad.

Only *I* knew that Mr. Gormulka had gotten access to a dangerous gadget just days before! And *I* was the one who had put it in his hands. If the world blew up that night, it would all be my fault.

If there was ever a time I had to prove my spy capabilities, it was tonight!

CHAPTER NINE

This was it. Even Dave the Monkey couldn't help Agent North now.

North stared down into the bottomless pit beneath him. He would only have one chance to jump over it. If a single thing went wrong, he was a goner. And if he didn't make the jump, the whole country was probably doomed.

But just "probably." Not definitely. Maybe Dr. Cringe would decide not to blow up the world. Maybe he'd have a change of heart and decide to give everyone in the world a free pony instead. It could happen! Maybe Dr. Cringe wasn't really so bad after all. Maybe he was just misunderstood. He did, after all, have excellent taste in suits.

Agent North knew he probably couldn't make the jump.

Was it safer not to try and just hope that Dr. Cringe would decide to have mercy on the world? Maybe he had been visited in the night by the Ghosts of Music Programs Past, Present, and Future and had decided to change his ways!

Agent North thought long and hard about simply turning around and joining in the card game that was going on back at his old classroom. If he was going to get blown up, shouldn't he just enjoy his last few minutes of being in one piece . . . ?

It's always weird being at school at night. I mean, I spend more time at school than I do at home most days, if you don't count the time that I'm in bed, which I don't. But when it's dark outside, school seems like a whole different place. And when you know you may not survive the night, well, that makes it even stranger.

My parents, Aunt Brianna, and Jack, who had gone back to sulking and acting like a real jerk, dropped me off at the door to my classroom.

About half the class, including Neil, Nicole, and Tony, were already there. During music programs, we all just hang out in our classrooms until it's time for our class to go to the auditorium.

As I had expected, as soon as I stepped into the room, everyone started making fun of my sweater.

"Check out North!" said Neil. "He's dressed like a four-year-old!"

A bunch of people laughed. Nicole grinned, then whispered something to the girl next to her, who started going around whispering to everyone else. I knew they were making fun of me. All of them. It was not the way I wanted to spend the last couple hours of my life.

But soon people stopped laughing and went back to just hanging out. Some people were sitting at their desks, drinking cups of that orange drink they're always passing around at school parties, and others were sitting on the floor, playing a card game called Bull Crap, where you have to lie your butt off to win. Playing it with Tony Zunker is always fun.

I didn't try to get in on the game. I had too much to worry about. I sat down at my desk and tried to figure out what I should do. Should I risk trying to get the calculator back, or just trust that when Mr. Gormulka made his move, Dad, Jack, and Dad's boss would probably take care of it?

Deep down, I knew I couldn't risk that. Dad, Jack, and Dad's boss didn't even know that Mr. Gormulka had the calculator. And I still had the key to Storage Room B, even though I was scared to death to go in there. What if Mr. Gormulka was waiting there to kill me? What if he had gotten his hands on *extra* sharks and spiders?

I looked around the room, trying to think up a plan.

If Mr. Gormulka was going to kill me, he wouldn't expect me to know about it. If I stuck around in the classroom, then went onstage with everyone else, he would know right where to find me. Maybe he'd be waiting in the wings to grab me right out of the line when we walked out to the risers! Or maybe he would be in the audience, waiting for me to come onstage before punching in the code that would make the calculator blow up the whole school!

Obviously, I couldn't go onstage. It wasn't safe. Not for me or anyone else. I had to get out of here. If I wasn't onstage, Mr. Gormulka might not blow us all up.

I walked up to Mr. Summers, who was at his desk, happily doing long division with a pencil.

"Are you okay, Andrew?" he asked. "Don't you want to play cards with everyone else?"

"I'm just nervous, I guess," I said. "Can I go to the bathroom?"

"Well, we're going onstage in a minute," he said. "I think you'd better wait."

I needed something to distract Mr. Summers enough that I could sneak out. And if anyone could create a disturbance like that, it was Ryan Kowalski.

I walked over to sit next to him. He was in the back with his feet on his desk, sipping an orange drink and wearing his usual white T-shirt with the sleeves rolled up. Mrs. Wellington would probably be mad at him for not wearing something nicer, but cool guys like Ryan don't care what people like her think.

"I have to get out of here," I said.

"I don't blame you," Ryan said. "It's a good thing for you you're my best customer. If you didn't buy so many insults from me, I'd really be letting you have it right now for that sweater!"

When you buy insults from Ryan Kowalski, you don't just get insults. You get protection!

"I know!" I said. "But that's not it. I've got to get out of this classroom. It's life or death!"

"Really?" he said. "You're that nervous about singing a solo?"

"It's worse than that," I said. "I think there's a good

chance Mr. Gormulka might be plotting to kidnap me while I'm going onstage and feed me to sharks!"

Ryan looked at me and raised an eyebrow.

"It's true!" I said. "I'm not sure about the sharks, but I'm almost sure that he's planning to murder me tonight. He might even try to blow up the whole school!"

Ryan laughed and ran his hand through his slicked-back hair. "You didn't think I was serious about that, did you?" he asked. "I've heard there are comic books in there, but I just made that other stuff up because Tony Zunker was there. I didn't think you'd *both* believe it!"

"But it's *true!*" I said. "I don't know exactly what's in that room, except for all the comic books, but I know that Mr. Gormulka guards it just as much as people say, and I have a good reason to think he's planning to kill me tonight. You've got to believe me!"

He shrugged, but I could tell he still thought it was funny. "Hey, man, if you're serious, I believe you," he said. "I told you, you hear some crazy stuff when you're on the inside. Nothing surprises me anymore."

"So I need to get out of here," I said. "It's not safe for *any-one* for me to be here. I just need a disturbance so I can sneak out of the room."

"You need someone to distract Mr. Summers?" he asked. "Piece of cake. Watch!"

He put his feet down, sat up, and raised his hand. He kept it up for a minute or so before Mr. Summers even noticed.

"Ryan?" he said. "Are you actually raising your hand before talking for once, now that we're not actually in class?"

"I just have a math question," said Ryan.

Mr. Summers's eyes lit up. It was almost like he had a lightbulb implanted in his brain that switched on every time someone mentioned math.

"Let me have it!" said Mr. Summers.

"Can you show me how to multiply fractions?" he asked. "I'm baking a cake tomorrow, but I'm only doing two-thirds of the recipe."

Mr. Summers jumped up from his seat. "Oh boy!" he said. "Multiplying fractions is really more of a sixth-grade thing— I *never* get to teach sixth-grade math!"

He ran up to the board, and Ryan leaned over to me. "I have a brother in sixth grade," he whispered, "and I looked through his math book. Any time you want to distract Mr. Summers, just ask him about something from the sixth-grade math book."

Mr. Summers began to draw all over the marker board, talking about a mile a minute. I'd hardly ever seen him so excited!

"Now, the bottom number in a fraction is the denominator," said Mr. Summers. "If it's easier for you to remember it by calling it the de-bottom-ator, go right ahead."

Ryan leaned over to me. "There you go," he said. "Run. He'll never notice!"

And I stood up and slipped out of the room. Anyone could have. Abraham Lincoln himself could have stepped into the room, given a speech, and left, and Mr. Summers probably wouldn't have noticed.

Ryan Kowalski is a genius! All that extra time he spent in the classroom was really paying off.

I ran out of the room and into the cool safety of the hallway. In a minute, they'd be lining everyone up to take the stage. When they couldn't find me, they'd probably think I was just too nervous to sing the solo.

Which was only partly true.

Someone else could handle it. They'd probably get Melvin Purvis in. That kid might be a dork, but he sure can sing. The only reason *he* didn't get to do the solo is that he didn't want to. He gets really nervous singing in public. But in an emergency, he'd probably step in. He'd nail the solo and everyone would think he was a hero. They wouldn't know that the *real* hero was a kid in a cutesy-wootsy sweater who had kept everyone from getting blown up. That's life as a spy for you! You never really get the credit you deserve.

I ran around the corner and hid out for a minute, listening to the sound of the first graders singing in the auditorium. Just as the second graders were going on, I heard the sound of my class being marched out of the classroom toward the auditorium, where they'd stand backstage until the last class of second graders was done singing. Someone was shouting, "Where's Andrew?" and someone else was saying, "Melvin can sing his part. He's a good singer!"

I knew my parents would probably freak out when they saw I wasn't onstage. Dad and Jack might even spring into action, run out into the halls, and get into a fight with Mr. Gormulka. That would be ideal, because I could probably use some backup.

A few seconds later, my class had gone by. Mr. Gormulka was probably backstage, wondering where that superspy he was going to kill had wandered off to. Ha! *It's not going to be that easy, Mr. G—if that is your real name!*

I had the whole school to myself. It was the perfect chance to get into Storage Room B and see if the calculator was still there. If I could nab it now, then by the time Mr. Gormulka even knew he'd been foiled, I'd be safely at home, trying to explain to my parents why I hadn't been onstage. I ran into the second-grade hall and up to the door to Storage Room B.

That's when I froze.

What if there really were booby traps in there? What if I got hit by a flying arrow or a death ray as soon as I stepped inside?

Then I heard it. Totally creepy whistling, coming from the next hallway. "The Pennsylvania Polka."

Mr. Gormulka!

It was too late to run. I felt all the blood drain from my face as he turned into the second-grade hall. He stopped whistling the second he saw me. This was it! I was shark food for sure!

"North!" he shouted. "I warned you not to be poking around here again!"

CHAPTER TEN

Agent North had used every gadget he had, even the monkey-poop cleaner. He had used up the batteries in the pants-dropping whistle to stop the robot guards. That had been a particularly lucky break: if those robots hadn't been wearing pants, North would have been a goner!

But now there were no more gadgets. Dave the Monkey was back in the flying car, trying to dismantle a bomb. There was no one left in the fortress but Agent North and the evil Dr. Cringe, who stared down at North with murderous eyes.

There was only one thing left to do.

Run!

"I . . . I wasn't going to the storage room," I said. "I just happened to be in the same hall."

Mr. Gormulka tossed his rag onto the floor and started running toward me. I could tell he was furious.

"Don't give me any nonsense, North!" said Mr. Gormulka. "You're in for it now!"

What could I do? I ran!

I turned back and took off at full speed. All the while, I could hear Mr. Gormulka chasing me. His footsteps echoed down the hall and mixed with the sound of the second graders singing in the auditorium.

I turned into the gym, trying to lose him, and ran clear over to the basketball hoop, but he followed me right in.

It was a dumb move. Now I was trapped! I stood beneath the basketball hoop, and Mr. Gormulka stood just inside the doorway. We stared at each other from across the gym, and I prayed that he didn't have some sort of laser watch that he could fire at me from where he was. I never should have run in here. There was only one way out, and Mr. Gormulka was blocking it.

At least it gave me a chance to look him over. The calculator was big enough that he couldn't have hidden it in his pocket, and he didn't seem to be carrying it. He must have left it in Storage Room B. At least I had *that* going for me.

"Get back here, North!" Mr. Gormulka said. "I warned you about going near that room."

I decided I had only one choice: pull evasive action. Jack

had taught me how to do that. I put my hands up, like I was surrendering, and started walking toward him.

"I give up," I said. "I'll go quietly."

"That's better," he said. And he started walking toward me, like he was going to meet me in the middle of the gym.

Once he was safely away from the door, I started running again. I ran right past him, out the door, and into the hall, slamming the door behind me.

I had turned into the next hall by the time I heard Mr. Gormulka running out of the gym. That gave me enough of a head start that I was home free, if I could just find a safe place to hide!

I kept running, right in the direction of the auditorium, hoping that Dad and Jack would spring out of nowhere with laser flamethrowers. But instead, Mrs. Wellington stepped out from around the corner. We both stopped running the second we saw her. Running in the halls in front of Mrs. Wellington was too risky even for Mr. Gormulka!

"Hank!" she said. "Where have you been? The program is half over, and the 'Donate Here' sign isn't up above the table. Get moving!"

"I have to deal with a student," he growled.

"Do it later!" said Mrs. Wellington. "That sign has to go up *now*. Come on!"

Mr. Gormulka grumbled, and Mrs. Wellington turned over to look at me.

"And you!" she said. "Hurry up! We've been looking everywhere for you!"

"I just had to tell Mr. Gormulka about the sign," I lied. It was probably the worst lie I ever told, but she was too busy freaking out to notice.

"Let Mr. Gormulka and me deal with that, you go get backstage! Let's go, Hank. The sign is in my office. After that, I'll need you to mop up the lobby quickly, before any parents come out. Their feet really scuffed up the floor on the way in!"

And they walked off toward the office. Mr. Gormulka shot me a dirty look, but I knew that he was going to be occupied for a few minutes. Mrs. Wellington wasn't going to let him out of her sight for the rest of the program. He might still be able to get the calculator out later and blow up the school before the program ended, but I was going to be safe for a few minutes! And there was no way he could kidnap me if I was onstage. I could make another run for Storage Room B after I sang. It looked like I'd be singing the solo after all!

I ran to the auditorium. The second graders were just finishing up, and my class was still lining up, ready to go onto the risers onstage. Nicole and Madison were standing off to the side, and Melvin was standing there with them, looking really, really nervous. He was wearing a really nice suit. If he'd gone on, Dad's boss might have thought he was me. But he didn't look as sharp as I would have looked in a suit as nice as his. He looked like he was going to be sick.

I ran up to where they were standing.

"Andrew!" said Melvin. "Where the heck were you?"

"I got a bit sidetracked," I said, cool as you please. "Sorry I'm late."

"I was going to go on in your place!" said Melvin. "Mr. Summers was panicking!"

"You want to sing the solo for me?" I asked. "You still can if you want to. You're better dressed for it than I am."

"No way!" said Melvin. "I've never been so glad to see anyone in my life! I was going to sue you if I had to sing the solo."

"All right," I said with a sigh. "I'll do it."

"And you'd better not screw up!" said Nicole.

I looked at her. What did she know? Why should I be nervous about singing a stupid song? I'd just escaped from a dangerous supervillain and maybe even saved her butt from getting blown to smithereens!

All of a sudden, I wasn't scared of singing anymore. In fact, I'd never felt so alive! I had escaped from Mr. Gormulka without a single spy gadget or monkey to help me. As Aunt Brianna would have said, I had been reborn!

A minute later, we were onstage. Madison, Nicole, and I stood in front, ready to go up to the microphone for the solos. Melvin stood on the risers with everyone else.

I looked out at the crowd and saw my whole family there. Aunt Brianna stood up and started cheering when the three of us stepped to the microphone for the solos in "Kids Are Music." I wondered which person was Dad's boss from the spy headquarters. Whoever he was, he was looking at a kid who'd just successfully escaped from an enemy spy!

Back behind them, I could see the lobby through the doors. Mr. Gormulka was out there, helping Mrs. Wellington put up the sign. So far, we were still safe.

When I stepped up to the microphone for my solo, I nailed every single note. I'd never done it better! We blew the crowd away, if I do say so myself. When the song ended, everyone cheered, and I stepped back onto the risers feeling like a million bucks. I didn't even mind the fact that I was wearing a stupid sweater or how stupid we must have looked singing "The Cornersville West Rap." I could have done the whole thing in a bunny suit and still felt like the coolest guy in town!

After the rap ended, we filed off the risers, right past Mr. Gormulka. I worried that he might grab me, but just before we got to him, Mrs. Wellington ran up to him.

Mr. Summers led us down the hall toward the class. We gave each other high fives on a job well done while Mrs. Kingfield's class walked onto the stage to sing "How You Gonna Keep 'Em Down on the Farm." While they sang, I sang it the way Todd did, and everyone cracked up until Mr. Summers told me to knock it off.

"Man," said Tony Zunker as we walked up to the classroom door, "I'm glad that's over!"

"Pretty cool, huh?" I asked.

"I'm sure glad you showed up, Andrew," said Melvin, who was right in front of me. "I really thought I was going to be sick!"

Melvin still looked pale, and he was sort of shivering.

"You still don't look so hot, man," said Tony. "It's over. Relax!"

"Yeah," I said. "You didn't eat the potato salad at lunch today, did you?"

"I had seconds of it," said Melvin.

"Not smart," I said. "You should never eat that stuff after Wednesday."

Then it happened. The only thing that *can* happen when you mix nervousness with Friday potato salad.

Melvin started shaking and coughing. He stepped out of the line, leaned his back against the wall, and puked. Right there in the hall!

"Ew!" shouted Nicole. "You almost puked on my shoes, you jerk!"

Mr. Summers jumped over the pile of puke to Melvin. "Are you okay, Melvin?" he asked.

"Of course he isn't!" said Ryan. "He just ralphed on the floor!"

But Melvin nodded. I could tell he was more embarrassed than anything else.

"Keep heading back to class, everybody," said Mr. Summers. "It's nothing to worry about. Someone pukes at the program every year."

Just then, I heard a high-pitched shriek. Mrs. Wellington was running up the hall.

"You see, Joyce?" said Mr. Summers. "You get the kids all worked up thinking the program is life and death, and every year someone gets sick!"

"I'm going to sue the school!" said Melvin.

Mrs. Wellington gave Mr. Summers a dirty look, then pulled out a walkie-talkie.

"Hank," she said into it, "we have a two-thirteen in the hall. Secure the doors and keep the parents from leaving the auditorium, then get out here and clean it up!"

She hustled us along, toward the room. A few seconds later, I saw Mr. Gormulka round the corner and rush toward a supply closet. Obviously he was going to be busy for a few minutes . . .

. . . which made this a perfect chance for me to get that calculator back!

"I think I got some puke on me!" I said, thinking on my feet. "I'd better go wash up." No one can stop you from going to the bathroom when you have puke on you. It's like sharpening your pencil when the lead is broken.

I ran down the hall, away from the class. Past the gym. Past the third-grade hall. Down into the second-grade hall and right up to Storage Room B!

I put the key into the keyhole, and this time, I didn't hesitate. I turned the key right away and opened the door. This was it! I was about to go into a room that no other kid in school history had ever gotten into and lived to tell the tale!

I never would have guessed what I'd see inside of it.

CHAPTERELEVEN

Dave the Monkey nodded, as if to say "Mission accomplished," as the door to the secret headquarters slowly opened. Dave couldn't talk, of course, but Agent North could tell what he was thinking just by looking into his intelligent monkey eyes.

"Great job, Dave," Agent North said. "Are you ready for this?"

Dave nodded, clapped his hands, and screeched.

The two of them stood before the open door to Dr. Cringe's secret headquarters. The quest was at an end, as long as they could get in and out without falling through any trapdoors.

Agent North took a cautious step into the room, looking around in shock at the shabby furniture and piles of junk. . . .

Storage Room B didn't look like an evil spy's headquarters at all. There was no shark tank. No spider pit. No booby traps at all, as far as I could tell. No arrows shot out at me when I stepped inside, and no trapdoors opened beneath my feet.

In fact, it looked more like a little apartment than anything else. There was an old orange armchair, a table, a stereo, and a microwave.

There were posters for polka bands on the walls. On the wall by the armchair was a poster with a bunch of guys who were dressed like Mega Mart cashiers, only with sillier hats. The logo on top said they were called Whoopee Norm Eddlebeck and the Dairyland Dutchmen. Another poster had a bunch of different bands on it. There was a logo on top for the Racine Polka Fest.

On one wall, there were a bunch of shelves. One of them was full of junk—old mittens and stuff. Stuff from the Lost and Found, probably. The top shelf held a bunch of toys, electronics, and other stuff that looked like it had been confiscated—including Jack's calculator!

The other shelves seemed to be covered with boxes and boxes of comic books. At least *that* rumor was true!

But I didn't see a supercomputer or anything. And certainly no dead bodies. I couldn't *smell* any bodies, either. All I smelled was stale popcorn.

Wow.

My first thought was *Boy, what an underachieving supervillain! Not a single booby trap!*

But then I came to my senses.

This was not Mr. Gormulka's secret headquarters. It was just a room where he hung out. He didn't kill people in here. He just listened to polka music and read comic books, from the looks of it.

For a second, I felt relieved. Even if I got caught, I was definitely going to live through the night. At worst, I'd probably just have to do indoor recess for a week for taking the key and breaking into the room.

But then I started to feel disappointed.

Everything Jack had told me was wrong!

Had he lied to me? Had he lied to me . . . about *every-thing*?

All of a sudden, I felt really stupid. Was it possible that Jack wasn't a spy at all? That he hadn't been ignoring me since he turned thirteen because he had to be all secretive? That he was just ignoring me because he had become a total jerk?

I didn't know what to think about it. I almost couldn't, because it hurt too much. But at the same time, these thoughts just kept coming at me.

Maybe that spot where the bodies were buried in the house down the street was just an old garden that had been overgrown by weeds. And when the lights were on in that abandoned house behind the cemetery on Bartleby Way, it probably wasn't ghosts, like Jack said. It was probably just re-altors, like Mom said. Why would ghosts even need to turn the lights on, anyway?

And Wayne Schneider probably wasn't an old rock star in disguise. He was probably just some fat guy who lived down the street.

I felt like I was going to be sick. In just a couple of seconds, I had gone from feeling like a superspy at the top of my game to feeling like a really dumb little kid.

Everything I'd ever believed was a lie!

Maybe Dad really *was* an insurance salesman. He didn't say "yeppers" just to throw people off. He actually said "yeppers." His boss, the one who had come to the program, really *was* the boss of the insurance company, not the boss of all the local international superspies. He'd probably never seen a real laser flamethrower in his life.

There was no secret chamber underneath our house that had a swimming pool, a gym, and a sauna, or any training facilities. Not even a tunnel to the spy headquarters.

And, worst of all, I wasn't going to be getting a monkey anytime soon.

I was so bummed, I couldn't even bring myself to run when I heard the sound of Mr. Gormulka's voice behind me.

"Well, you did it, North," he said calmly. He sounded mad, but not like he was going to attack me or anything. "No other kid has ever got in here before. Your brother tried to about a hundred times. How did you get it unlocked?"

I turned around and looked at him. He was still holding his mop. He didn't look nearly so murderous anymore. He just looked like a regular mild-mannered janitor with a scar above his eyebrow.

"I found a copy of the key this afternoon," I said. "Sorry about that."

"I could suspend you for life for taking that," he said. "But now that you've seen inside, I guess I'd better not, huh?"

I looked over at him, wondering what the heck he could mean. Surely he wasn't going to kill me because I'd seen his comic books and polka posters! "Why not?" I asked.

"I guess you were probably expecting to see dead bodies or piles of money or something in here?" he asked. "Those dumb rumors just won't die."

I shrugged. I didn't want to look as stupid as I felt.

"It's just where I keep all my stuff," he said casually. "My wife hates polka music. Won't let me play it in the house. And she doesn't like me wasting my money on comic books, so I have to keep my collection hidden in here. I have to be really careful not to let anyone see it. If the teachers knew, it would probably get back to my wife. She and Coach Walker have tea together all the time. And then I'd be in big trouble!"

"So that's why you won't let anyone see this room?" I asked.

"Yep," he said. "No dead bodies or anything. Just the stuff I don't want my wife to know about."

I took another look around, feeling like a real idiot. I was just Jack's very own version of Tony Zunker. He was probably just telling me these lies to see if I'd believe them. He probably remembered that Mr. Gormulka went around whistling polka music and just made up that story about Will Hannon so I'd be freaked out if I heard him whistling!

I felt like the most gullible person alive.

"I think I'd better get back to the classroom," I said.

"Not so fast," said Mr. Gormulka. "I ought to give you in-door recess or detention, at least, for snooping around where you're not allowed. But I'd rather just have you promise me that you won't tell anyone what's really in here. If anyone asks, tell them some story about dead bodies or something. My wife's already heard that one."

I shrugged. "I *guess* I can keep my mouth shut," I said, "but can I have the calculator back? The one that got taken up yesterday?"

"Is that all you were after?" said Mr. Gormulka. "You're getting it back on Monday, anyway."

"I know," I said. "But it's my brother's. I wasn't supposed to take it. And he needs it tomorrow."

"Fair enough, I guess," said Mr. Gormulka. "I wouldn't want your brother to flunk out of whatever grade he's in now because of me."

He walked over to the top shelf, took the calculator down, and handed it to me. "Here," he said. "Promise you won't tell anyone what's in here?"

"I promise," I said.

"And I'll take the key back, too," he said.

I handed it over to him.

"Just don't let me catch you snooping around again,

okay?" he said. "When your brother and that Mark Brueggen kid were poking around, people started thinking this place was some kind of Chamber of Secrets or something. I don't wanna go through that again!"

"Okay," I said. "I'll be quiet."

"Good," he said. "Now get back to your class."

And I walked out of the room, back to my classroom.

When I had left to break into that room, I had been Andrew "Danger" North, superspy.

But when I walked back into class, I was just regular old Andrew North.

When Neil came up and said, "Nice job on the solo, An-*dy*," I didn't even have the energy to call him a cheese bag.

CHAPTER TWELVE

Agent North had never felt so down. All his life, all he had
wanted to do was be a spy. He had been training since he was
six. And now he was going to have to go back to being a regular kid, just like everyone else. Just a regular kid with messy hair
and no pet monkey. No flying car or pants-dropping whistle, either. It was a lot to get used to. He had planned to be a spy until he was an old man. But now his plans had been thwarted.

Perhaps he could join a polka band. . . .

Through the intercom, we could hear the fifth graders singing, which meant the show was just about over. Once they finished, Mrs. Wellington would probably make a speech asking everyone to donate money to the school. Then they'd open the doors and let our parents come get us.

I sat at my desk and opened Jack's calculator. No one had messed with it. When I turned it on, the message I'd typed in the day before came up. I pushed a button marked CLEAR and it disappeared.

I breathed a sigh of relief. If Jack had found that message, he wouldn't just be mad that I'd used his calculator—he'd also probably laugh at how stupid I'd been.

A few minutes later, Mom, Dad, Jack, and Aunt Brianna picked me up, and we all went out for ice cream at the ice cream shop on Venture Street. But I still felt depressed. When even ice cream doesn't make you feel better, you know you've got problems.

While we ate, we listened to Aunt Brianna go on and on about how the music really spoke to her and how she just had to find a recording of "Hello Central, Give Me No Man's Land." She said she was going to start collecting old parlor songs and become a real expert. Mom said it would go great next to her collections of cookie jars, antique buttons, plates with cartoon characters on them, and Raggedy Ann stuff.

I tried to act happy, but I couldn't even look at Jack. And I realized for the first time that my dad wasn't acting like a dork to throw people off. He was just kind of a dork, plain and simple.

But then, when we were about halfway through with our ice cream, Mr. Cunyan walked in with a guy wearing a suit. A *sharp-looking* guy. His hair was perfect. He totally looked like a spy.

"Well, Jim!" said the guy, walking over to us. "Fancy meeting you here!"

"Hi, Ward!" said Dad. "Everyone, this is Ward, my boss."

Everyone waved. It was weird. Dad's boss looked just like I imagined he would when I thought he was the head of a spy company.

"And I believe you know Mr. Cunyan," said Dad's boss, pointing to Mr. Cunyan. "Especially this guy!"

He pointed at me, and I smiled as best I could.

"You did a bang-up job on that solo," said Dad's boss. "I was very impressed."

"You were great!" said Mr. Cunyan. "Mrs. Wellington probably won't put me on cafeteria duty for life after all!"

"Yeppers," said Dad as he put his hand on my shoulder. "We're very proud of him. Would you two care to join us?"

"Oh, I'm afraid we can't," said Dad's boss. "We have important business to discuss!"

He winked at Dad, and the two of them walked over to a booth at the other end of the ice cream shop.

It suddenly occurred to me that something strange was going on. Not counting Mrs. Wellington, people don't go around winking unless they're up to something.

Obviously, Mr. Gormulka wasn't really a supervillain. Jack had been lying about that.

But Dad's boss sure *looked* like a spy to me.

And why would *any* life insurance company insure Mr. Cunyan? The guy looked like he might die if someone snuck up behind him and yelled. They'd lose money on that deal for sure. I had forgotten about that!

And, anyway, Dad still couldn't have talked me into eating peas. He couldn't *really* be an insurance salesman!

Then I remembered the secret decoder rings. If they were just prizes from a cereal box, why would he still have them? It's not like cereal companies go around sending secret messages to grown-ups.

All of a sudden, I understood why Dad's boss had just winked at us like that. Mr. Cunyan probably worked as a spy! They weren't over there discussing insurance, they were talking about important spy stuff!

Maybe there was a coded message built into the music at the program. That explained Mr. Cunyan's obsession with these weird parlor songs and that silly rap he wrote. When we were up there singing stupid songs, we were actually sending out secret messages!

The man was a genius!

When I thought it over, it all made sense. The whole day had been one big test for me!

Dad's boss must have gotten the message I'd sent on the calculator after all, then heard that the calculator was in Storage Room B from Mr. Cunyan, who'd heard it from Tony during class.

Then he must have decided that seeing if I could get it

back would be a good test for me. He probably asked Jack to tell me a lot of scary stuff about Mr. Gormulka so I'd *think* I was on a life-or-death mission. They wouldn't make me go on a *real* dangerous mission without the proper gadgets, but by making me *think* I was on a dangerous mission, they got to see how I acted under pressure. It was brilliant!

Coach Walker was probably in on it, too. The reason she'd gotten me in trouble was to give me a chance to get the spare key and retrieve the calculator!

All the pieces fit!

I was beginning to feel like Andrew "Danger" North again. I had just passed a test—and with flying colors! I'd broken into Storage Room B, retrieved a gadget that I'd thought was going to blow up the world, escaped from a guy who I thought was a dangerous villain, *and* nailed the solo, all in one night. And Dad's boss, the head of the spy headquarters, had been very impressed! He'd said so himself. I'd probably get the call to go pro any day!

I finished my ice cream feeling like a king.

They'd almost had me going for a minute there—I'd really believed that Dad and his boss actually *did* sell insurance. They were clever, but not clever enough for me!

When we finished our ice cream, Aunt Brianna walked over to Mr. Cunyan's booth to ask him where she could find out more about parlor songs, and they ended up talking for about ten minutes. While they chatted, Dad and his boss whispered to each other, all secretive-like. Talking about me, probably.

That night, back at home, I knocked on Jack's door.

"Yeah?" he called out from inside.

"I found your calculator," I said.

He opened the door, and I handed it to him.

"Thank God," he said. "Where was it?"

"It was under some magazines in the living room," I lied. "You must have left it there yesterday."

"Well, thanks," he said, taking it from me. "And nice job on the solo tonight. I wouldn't have had the guts to do that when I was your age. Or now, for that matter."

"Thanks!" I said. "And by the way, I know you were making up all that stuff about Mr. Gormulka."

Jack smiled. "No I wasn't," he said. "He's totally a dangerous spy. You're lucky you survived the night!"

"You can drop the act," I said. I knew I'd made a promise to Mr. Gormulka, but since Jack was a spy, I knew he'd keep this quiet. "Storage Room B is just where Mr. Gormulka hides his comic books and polka records from his wife. I snuck in after the program."

"What?" asked Jack. "You actually got into Storage Room B?"

"Sure," I said casually. I could see he was totally impressed. Mr. Gormulka had said that Jack had never made it in there.

"Nice going!" he said. "I spent my whole time in elementary school trying to get into that room, and I never managed it! How the heck did you get in?"

"I took the spare key off Mr. Gormulka's tool belt earlier today and snuck in while he was busy cleaning up some puke," I said.

"Awesome!" he said.

"Hey," I said. "I couldn't have done it if you hadn't taught me all those skills."

I winked at him and he nodded.

I turned up the volume on his stereo so that if his room was bugged, no one would be able to hear us talking over the music.

"Look," I whispered. "I know you aren't allowed to talk about your job. But do you think you can put in a good word for me?"

Jack smirked a bit, like he was going to laugh at me. For a second, I felt like an idiot all over again. But then he gave me a really fast salute.

"You got it, kid," he said.

I was feeling so slick, I went back to my room and put on the suit that was hanging in my closet. Mom was wrong. It wasn't too small for me at all. It fit like a dream, and when I checked myself out in the mirror, I looked totally sharp. And even though it was the end of a long, busy day, my hair was perfect.

Any day now, I'll open my locker and find a note asking me to meet up with Mr. Cunyan and Coach Walker at that weird statue of the naked angel on a tricycle at the mall. They'll pick the angel's nose or scratch his butt or something, and that will open up a secret passage into a spy office, where they'll give me a couple of gadgets, have me fill out some paperwork, and maybe give me my first paycheck in advance.

I'll be making enough cash to buy a monkey in no time and a whole pile of Ryan's insults!

I felt a lot better when I went to bed that night. There's always a chance that Jack is still just making things up, but the only theory that makes any sense to me is that he, Dad, Mr. Cunyan, and Coach Walker are spies. And Jack was being nice again, at least a little, so maybe he really wasn't such a jerk after all.

It still seems a bit weird. But weird stuff is always happening in Cornersville Trace!

And the next morning, when I walked down the street, I could have sworn I heard the sound of an electric guitar blasting out of Wayne Schneider's garage.

ADAM SELZER

is the author of the novels *How to Get Suspended
and Influence People*, *Pirates of the Retail Wasteland*,
and *I Put a Spell on You*, as well as a forthcoming work of
nonfiction, *The Smart Aleck's Guide to American
History*. He grew up in the suburbs of Des Moines and now
lives in downtown Chicago, where he can write in a
different coffee shop every day without even leaving his
neighborhood. In addition to his work as a tour guide and
assistant ghostbuster (really), he moonlights as a rock star.
Check him out at www.adamselzer.com.